MOONLIGHT PROMENADE

A TIMELESS AFFAIR

LILLIANA ROSE

BLURB

I never believed time travel was possible.

Until a mysterious pendant transported me to Victorian London, where I'm hunted by dark creatures known as shadows, beings that drain my energy and stalk my every move.

That's when I learned monsters *are* real.

Lord Nathaniel Blackwood is cursed—caught mid-transformation between man and werewolf, shunned by high society. But not all monsters are evil, and Nathaniel might be the only one who can help me survive.

Our forbidden attraction sparks a fire I can't control. I'm trapped in the past and drawn into a future I never imagined—where every touch is a risk, and every whispered word could cost me my life.

If Nathaniel and I can uncover who's behind the shadows and their twisted purpose, I might have a chance to return to my own time.

But the longer I stay, the more I want to remain —no matter the danger or who wants the pendant… or me.

CHAPTER 1

$\mathcal{E}$mily

The faded script writhed before my eyes, a jumble of archaic jargon clung to its secrets like a shroud. I gnawed on the rim of my chipped mug, the lukewarm tea doing nothing to quench the growing unease in my gut.

Outside, the London night pulsed with a life I felt increasingly detached from, a distant siren wailed in the gloom, thumping bass music from some first-year's party, the odd yells and screams, and even the hiss of cats fighting.

But tonight, the silence was different.

It hummed with a low, predatory thrum as if

something unseen was watching and waiting. I pushed the thought away, telling myself it was just the stress, yet the hair on my neck prickled in warning.

The rattle of the door sent a jolt of adrenaline through me. A shadow flickered outside the grimy window, and I caught a glimpse of something unnatural moving in the darkness outside. A wolf standing as if human?

I shook my head, trying to dispel the creeping unease and focus on the precarious stacks of family history surrounding me. I wanted answers which was why I worked late in my office, in the attic space at the University College of London.

I flipped open another page of my father's journal, and a drawing caught my eye—one I had previously overlooked. It depicted a wolf standing upright, clad in a tailored suit from the mid-1800s. The image was striking, a seamless blend of man and beast, exuding elegance and primal power. The drawing had a haunting beauty, igniting a mix of attraction and curiosity I couldn't ignore.

The phone's shrill ring sliced through the quiet, making me jump. Caller ID flashed 'Mom.' I pressed my lips together, already bracing myself.

Answering meant a familiar battle, a tug-of-war between her anxieties and my insatiable curiosity. I let it ring, the insistent trill grating on my nerves, mirroring the unease churning in my gut.

Finally, on the fifth ring, I relented and sighed as I tapped the answer button.

"Emily." Mom's voice was tight, strained with an emotion I recognized as a blend of worry and frustration. "It's late, you should be home."

I rubbed my temples, the pressure behind my eyes a constant companion these days. "Just finishing up."

"Finishing what, Emily? Another dead end? Another family secret that will only bring you more heartache?" The sharpness in her voice was a thin veil over the fear I knew she harbored.

"This is different," I insisted, my voice rising in defiance. "This is about Dad, and I won't end up like him."

Silence hung heavily between us, thick with unspoken grief. My father's death, barely six months ago, had left a gaping hole in my life, a void I desperately tried to fill with fragments of his past. His final months had been a descent into paranoia, a brilliant mind consumed by whispers of werewolves and ancient curses.

We'd dismissed it as dementia. But a part of me—a small, persistent voice—whispered that perhaps he hadn't been crazy. Perhaps he'd been afraid. But werewolves weren't real, right? Even here alone, I would question anything.

"Emily." Mom's voice softened, laced with a pleading tone. "He was ill. You know that. Don't let his obsession become yours. You have a future and a life to live. Don't waste it chasing ghosts."

"This isn't about ghosts, Mom. It's about understanding," I argued, my fingers tracing the faded ink below the drawing of the standing werewolf, the date 1848, and the initials 'NB' mocking me with its unanswered questions if such a beast could exist. Of course, it couldn't.

"Understanding won't bring him back," she countered, her voice laced with a weariness I felt mirrored in my soul. "Promise me you'll let it go, Emily. For your own sake."

"I can't," I whispered, the words barely audible even to my ears as I ended the call.

I pushed away from the desk, the chair scraping against the wooden floor. The near full moon, a malevolent eye peering through the grimy attic window, cast long, distorted shadows across the room. I remembered a crisp autumn evening years ago here looking out the same window with my father. The moon, full and bright, had painted the room in an ethereal glow. I'd been fascinated, reaching out a small hand toward the celestial orb.

"Don't," he'd said, his voice unusually sharp, pulling me back. He'd held me close, his grip tight, his breath warm against my ear. "The full moon holds ancient power. It can awaken things best left asleep." His eyes were wide, reflecting the moonlight with an unsettling intensity. "On nights like these, stay inside, away from the windows. The light can reveal things we're not meant to see."

A shiver ran down my spine, the memory vivid and unsettling. I pushed the thought away, focusing on the task at hand. I needed answers that lay buried in the mountain of documents before me.

A sharp rap at the door startled me. I hadn't heard anyone coming up the creaking stairs. My heart raced as I crossed the room, anticipation thrumming in my veins. Opening the door, I was met by a young man in a nondescript uniform, his expression a mix of fatigue and impatience. He held out a small, wooden box as if eager to be rid of it.

"Delivery for Emily Warren," he said.

My hand trembled as I accepted the parcel, my heart pounding. The unassuming box felt unexpectedly heavy, its weight unsettling and brimming with unspoken secrets. The label bore my name and university address, confirming it was meant for me —no mistake.

"Who..." I began, but the man had already

vanished into the night. I shut the door firmly as if sealing it could keep the darkness outside at bay.

I placed it on the desk and traced my fingers over the rough, aged paper, a sense of history emanating from it, as if it carried the whispers of generations past. With a surge of anticipation, I ripped away the paper to reveal a wooden box adorned with intricate carvings of wolves, full moons, and crossed arrows.

Hesitantly, I lifted the lid. Nestled on faded red velvet was a tarnished silver pendant, its surface intricately carved with two crossed arrows framing the shadowy silhouette of a wolf.

A gasp escaped my lips. It was the symbol of the wolf hunters, the very same depicted in the faded notes of my father's journal.

The wolf's fierce and alert silhouette was framed by the crossed silver arrows, their tips gleaming dully in the dim light, poised as if for the kill. This was the emblem of their relentless pursuit, a chilling blend of cunning and lethal precision—a mark of the Silver Brotherhood.

Whispers of the ancient order echoed in my memory. Tales of hunters bound by a sacred oath to protect humanity from the lurking threat of werewolves, their moonlit rituals veiled in secrecy, their silver weapons gleaming in the night as they stood vigilant against the darkness that prowled the woods.

But who would send me this? And why?

The pendant seemed to shimmer, a subtle glow emanating from its intricately carved surface. I reached for it, feeling the cool metal against my fingertips.

Holding it up to the moonlight, I gasped. The pendant pulsed gently, radiating a soft, ethereal light that illuminated the shadows around me. The glow intensified, bathing my hands in a silvery hue. It felt alive, as if it were responding to the moon above, the energy flowing through me like a current.

In a moment of desperation, I clutched the pendant and pressed it against my heart. A sudden warmth spread from the silver, chasing away the chill of the night air.

"What do you want me to see?" I whispered, a plea for the pendant to reveal its secrets.

The silver flickered, and a surge of ancient, powerful energy washed over me. My father's warnings echoed in my mind, his hushed tones speaking of the moon and its hidden mysteries.

"Reveal the truths hidden in shadows," I murmured, the words feeling both foreign and familiar on my tongue.

The pendant pulsed with light, bathing the room

in an ethereal glow. Driven by the urgent need for answers, I returned to the box. Beneath the velvet, a folded note lay waiting. My father's distinctive script was instantly recognizable. A knot of dread and anticipation tightened in my chest.

My fingers trembled as I unfolded the brittle paper. The words, penned in his familiar hand, seemed to sear themselves onto the page:

Emily, if you're reading this, I am gone. But I have set things in motion, things I couldn't finish. The pendant is the key, and I'm giving it to you now. It will lead you to the truth, to the heart of our family's legacy. You are stronger than you know. Trust your instincts. And beware the Moonlight Promenade.

The note trembled in my hand, the weight of his words a heavy burden. Where was the Moonlight Promenade? And why was Dad sending me a cryptic message from beyond the grave? Was this a warning?

The box was empty save for the note. Then I remembered the entry in my father's journal, the one referencing the wolf hunters' symbol.

Clutching the pendant, I raced to find the journal, frantically flipping through the worn pages until I found the passage. There, in his handwriting, were instructions on how to use the pendant.

A phrase from the journal, previously dismissed

as nonsensical, now flashed in my mind with sudden clarity.

"By the light of the moon, the past shall awaken," I whispered the words, my voice barely audible. As they left my lips, the pendant pulsed violently, sending ripples of energy through the air.

The room shimmered, shadows twisting and merging as if imbued with life. Fear and anticipation warred within me. The attic walls seemed to dissolve, and I felt myself drawn into a vortex of light, the very fabric of time bending around me.

The pendant's cool metal contrasted sharply with the sudden heat flooding my skin. Dizziness washed over me, and the room tilted as if caught in a storm.

A vivid, terrifying vision exploded in my mind— a cobbled street drenched in moonlight, shadowy figures swirling in the mist, and the chilling howl of a wolf echoing through the night.

Then, darkness.

I gasped, stumbling back against the desk, the pendant gripped tightly in my hand. My heart raced, pounding against my ribs, the vision so vivid and visceral that it left me trembling, the air thick with a palpable energy.

An invisible force pulled me away from the room, awakening something deep within me. My pulse roared in protest, and I opened my mouth to scream, but no sound escaped my lips.

My vision blurred, and colors swirled together before spiraling outward. I fought against the growing force that beckoned me toward the surge of energy, but it was too late.

I had already crossed the threshold, and the shadows of the past were reaching for me, hungry and insistent.

CHAPTER 2

*E*mily

The moment I stepped through the shimmering veil of time, the world around me shifted violently. Coal smoke and damp earth mingled in the air, while the clatter of horses' hooves against cobblestones echoed like a heartbeat in my ears. I stumbled, disoriented, my heart racing as I took in my surroundings of a bustling market square alive with vendors shouting their wares in a chaotic symphony.

Where the fuck was I?

People stared, their eyes widening as I stood frozen, caught between disbelief and awe. I glanced down at my clothes—modern and out of place in jeans and a T-shirt.

The women around me wore flowing skirts and shawls wrapped tightly around their shoulders, while the men sported waistcoats and plain trousers. This wasn't normal.

What had I been thinking, stepping into that light? Had it been a portal? That was the stuff of fantasy stories, not real life.

I clutched the pendant and then hung it around my neck, thinking it was the safest place for it. It's cool metal anchored me amid the whirlwind of chaos surrounding me.

A palpable energy pulsed from it in time with my heartbeat, binding us together and whispering that it was the very force that had opened the portal I had stepped through.

Fearful glances from those passing by caused my skin to prickle. I couldn't shake the feeling of being watched, like a stranger in a world that knew I didn't belong.

I moved deeper into the square, weaving through the crowd. The colors were richer, the sounds more vivid. The world pulsed with life in a way I had never experienced. I caught snippets of conversation, fragments of gossip floating around me like smoke.

"Have you heard about Lord Blackwood?" a woman whispered to her companion, clutching a basket of vegetables as if it were a shield. "The curse that keeps him in the form of a werewolf…"

I froze, the words striking a chord deep within me. Werewolf?

My father's ramblings echoed in my mind—curses and ancient fears. Had he come here? Was this what he had been warning me about?

As I wandered, a chill crept in, not just from the autumn air but from the unsettling sensation of being watched. Shadows flickered at the edges of my vision, and I caught glimpses of figures lurking in the alleys, their faces obscured yet their gazes sharp and unyielding. Were they following me?

My father's paranoia flashed in my mind, a symptom of his early dementia. Had he lost his grip on reality simply by coming to this place? Was this to be my future too?

I quickened my pace, cobblestones beneath my feet, each step pulling me deeper into a world where I didn't belong. I didn't want to end up like my dad—mad and confused, the lines of reality and fantasy blurred.

But how could I stop this?

Maybe if I uncovered the secrets he had sought, I could save myself. Yet that hope felt thin and fragile as I wandered aimlessly through the lengthening shadows that seemed to hungrily reach out for me.

Then something white caught my eye, fluttering in the cold afternoon breeze. I bent down, snatching up a newspaper, the date glaring back at me—1848.

This isn't possible.

Yet when I looked up, the streets were devoid of cars, only horse-drawn carts rattling by, no signs of planes or electrical wires. I was sure I was still in London.

"Best be careful, miss," an elderly man warned as I passed, his clouded eyes sharp with an intensity that made my skin prickle. "The moon brings out creatures of the dark. You'd do well to stay indoors come nightfall."

His words hovered in the air, heavy with unspoken dread. The pendant pressed against my chest, a constant reminder of my connection to this place and my family's legacy.

I couldn't stay here. I had to find a way back to the safety of my research office, my own time, and where I belonged. I might study genealogy and the past, but now that I was here, I longed for the familiar comforts of my own life. I hurried across the road, trying to return the way I had come as if that would provide my way home.

"Get out of the way!" a gruff voice growled.

A horse neighed, its high-pitched whinny filled with fear, and I turned just in time to see the whites of its eyes flashing at me. My feet stumbled, unable to coordinate in the chaos. Suddenly, the horse kicked me hard in the thigh, sending me sprawling onto the cobbled road.

Pain shot through my leg, sharp and immediate, as I landed heavily on my backside. I gasped, struggling to catch my breath. I wouldn't have to worry about getting back to my own time if I ended up dead.

"You all right, miss?" asked a young boy with a grubby face, peering down at me with wide eyes. "You gotta watch out for the toffs when they come through, you know."

I grimaced as I shifted, trying to assess my injury. The ache in my thigh was deep. I sensed a bruise already forming beneath my denim jeans. I didn't think the bone was broken.

"I'm fine," I managed, though my voice wavered. I wasn't, but the only person I could trust right now was myself.

The boy nodded, his expression softened. "They don't care much for folks like us. You gotta be quick on your feet."

I pushed myself up, wincing as I put weight on my injured leg. "Thanks for the tip," I said, trying to sound more composed than I felt. The shadows around me seemed to deepen, a reminder of the danger lurking at the edges of this unfamiliar world.

I glanced around, trying to regain my bearings, to see if there was a clear way forward. It wasn't that easy, of course.

The streets were bustling, but I felt isolated as if the crowd was moving in slow motion while I was trapped in a moment of panic. I had to keep moving to find a way back before the shadows closed in.

I limped forward, each step sending jolts of pain through my thigh, but I pressed on. The weight of uncertainty loomed over me, but I couldn't let fear paralyze me.

I ducked into a small apothecary shop, thinking it could provide the sense of safety I needed. The scent of dried herbs and pungent spices wrapped around me like a cloak.

The shopkeeper glanced up from behind a cluttered counter, suspicion etched deep into his furrowed brow.

"Can I help you?" he asked, a hint of wariness in his tone.

"I'm… just looking," I managed, my voice quivering as I scanned the shelves lined with jars of strange concoctions, each labeled in faded cursive script. I felt like a ghost in this world, an intruder carefully treading through the remnants of history.

As I turned to leave, a flicker of movement caught my eye in the reflection of a glass jar—someone standing just outside, watching me with an intensity that made my breath hitch. I stepped back, the floor creaking ominously behind me.

Through the glass, I saw him, a tall figure cloaked in shadows, his features obscured but unmistakable. His eyes glowed with a feral light, sharp and penetrating, and I was frozen in place for a moment.

He was no ordinary man, even though he wore a tailored suit. There was something wild about him, a presence that sent a shiver down my spine. The faint outline of fur bristled along his jawline, and as he shifted slightly, I caught the glint of elongated canines as they peeked from beneath his lips.

"Stay away!" I blurted, my voice trembling. The stories flared to life in my mind of a man tormented by a curse, doomed to hunt under the full moon. The weight of his gaze felt like a physical force, and I instinctively reached for the pendant around my neck. Its cool metal was a reminder of my connection to this world.

He paused, tilting his head, and for a fleeting moment, I thought I saw a flicker of recognition in his eyes. It was as if he could sense my fear, my confusion, and beneath it all, an unexplainable thread of connection. Was it possible that he, too, felt the pull of something beyond this cursed existence?

He growled softly, a low rumble that resonated deep within my chest. I took a step back, my heart pounding against my ribcage. This wasn't just a chance encounter. It felt like fate had drawn us together, two lost souls caught in the tumult of time.

Then, in a heartbeat, he turned and retreated into the street, leaving only the echo of his presence lingering in the air. I stood frozen, the weight of the moment pressing down on me. I had to uncover the truth about this man—this creature—if I was to understand the secrets that bound our fates.

I needed answers to understand why I was here and what awaited me. The whispers of the townsfolk echoed in my mind, intertwining with my father's warnings. I was part of something larger, entwined in a web of fate that spun beneath the surface of this seemingly ordinary world.

With a renewed sense of urgency, I stepped out of the shop and back into the square, the vibrant life around me both exhilarating and terrifying. I had to navigate this strange landscape to uncover the truth buried within my lineage before the shadows closed in on me completely.

CHAPTER 3

*L*ord Nathaniel Blackwood

What was she doing here?

The moment I caught sight of her, a jolt rippled through me. Her clothes—jeans and a T-shirt—screamed of a time I couldn't fathom, and the faint scent of the future clung to her like a shroud, overpowering and strange.

I straightened my jacket, forcing myself to walk with an air of calm dignity down the cobbled street, though the shadows felt thicker than usual.

Of course, it was because of her. They sensed her time-traveling energy and wanted to feed on her.

I should help her. The thought flickered through my mind like a flame, bright and inviting.

But I didn't turn back. I couldn't.

She wasn't the first to come through from the future. None lasted long, and I figured the same would happen to her. Yet this time, an unfamiliar guilt gnawed at me, a reaction to the way she'd looked at me through the glass.

Her gaze had stirred something deep within, awakening a desire I'd denied myself for so long, ever since the witch had cursed me.

As I strolled through the market square, the crowd's murmur washed over me. Vendors hawked their wares, and the scent of fresh bread mingled with the pungent aroma of herbs from nearby stalls. I nodded at a few familiar faces, their respect for me as Lord Blackwood evident but cold. There was no warmth in their acknowledgment, only the forced recognition of my title.

"Good day, my Lord," a merchant said, his voice low and deferential as I passed. He was a stout man, his hands callused from years of labor. I offered a curt nod in response, the weight of my title pressing down on me, more like my curse to be in both wolf and human form at once. "Lord Blackwood," he continued, hesitating for a moment. "The full moon will rise soon. Best keep your distance, sir."

I glanced upward, the sky darkening toward night. The sight bothered me, a constant reminder of my curse and the beast lurking beneath the surface that couldn't fully transform.

"I appreciate your concern," I replied, my tone clipped, and I continued on my way as if I needed to be warned. People didn't realize I wasn't a threat, they only saw me stuck between human and wolf, which scared them to the bone. Besides, the moon wasn't full yet.

As I moved through the throng, I noticed their furtive glances, the way they whispered behind their hands. I was a figure of intrigue and fear, a man burdened by a fate no one could understand. But the look of that woman in the apothecary—so bewildered, so lost— haunted me.

The familiar pull of the wolf within thrummed through my veins and urged me to protect her. But my instincts had been dulled by years of restraint, shackled by the witch's spell.

Would I allow her to become entangled in my fate?

The shadows lengthened around me as the sun dipped lower, and the weight of the approaching night grew heavy on my shoulders. I couldn't afford to get close to her.

I turned a corner, my heart heavy with conflict,

and caught a glimpse of her again, standing at the square's edge, looking lost and vulnerable. My instincts screamed to approach, to shield her from the dangers lurking in the twilight.

Instead, I paused, my breath catching in my throat. She was not a lost soul from another time but a fleeting moment, a reminder of what I couldn't have.

And so I walked on, the shadows whispering secrets around me, the full moon rising ever higher in the night sky, casting its cold light on a world that felt more isolated than ever. If I didn't get home soon, I would be hunted for simply being out.

As I walked through the market, the scent of spices filled the air, grounding me for a moment. But then a familiar scent wafted past, one that sent me spiraling into a memory I couldn't shake.

It was a moonlit night, much like this one, when I first met her father. The atmosphere was thick with tension, the air buzzing with unspoken words. I had slipped into the nearby tavern, desperate for a moment of respite from the shadows that clung to me. The flickering candles cast dancing shadows on the walls, and laughter mingled with hushed whispers.

Then I saw him—an older man with a rugged demeanor, his eyes sharp and observant. He was seated at a corner table, a drink in hand, and the moment our gazes locked, I felt an inexplicable connection.

"This doesn't look like a place you should be in," he said, his voice gravelly yet warm as I approached him. I could see the concern in his eyes, a flicker of something deeper beneath the surface.

"I needed a drink," I replied, keeping my tone neutral. "May I join you?"

He nodded, and I sat opposite him, curious to hear his story. "You're Lord Blackwood," he echoed, a knowing smile creeping onto his lips, chasing away the fear in his eyes. He kept looking around as if something was going to come for him. I'd never seen someone so on edge.

I clenched my fists under the table, hating when others knew more about me than I of them. "My reputation precedes me, unfortunately."

"Protect those you care about. Don't let your curse define you," he said, his gaze unwavering. What did that even mean? Then he started talking gibberish, his confusion clear. Before I could offer my help, he was gone.

The memory faded, but the weight of his words lingered in my mind, now suddenly having meaning. Protect those you care about. I shook my head, trying to dispel the fog of nostalgia that threatened to engulf me. That was the only time I had seen him.

Just then, a group of men brushed past, their laughter harsh and mocking. "Better watch out, Blackwood," one of them sneered, casting a wary glance in my direction. "We saw the werewolf hunters sharpening their knives down by the docks. They might mistake you for a rogue wolf, unable to control your abilities."

Their words struck like a blow, a reminder of my past missteps. I had broken the rules of the humans who ruled this land, defying the delicate balance between our worlds. The price had been steep, and I had paid it dearly with my freedom, my curse.

The urgency of the present clawed at my chest. I couldn't afford to let my instincts take over, not with her here. Yet, as the wolf within me stirred, urging me to protect her, I felt the weight of my history, the guilt, and the curse binding me to a fate I desperately sought to escape.

My jaw clenched as shabbily dressed boys darted through the encroaching dusk, their torches coaxing the gas lamps to life. With each sputtering flame, the sunlight retreated further, and the city's corners grew indistinct, swallowed by the advancing gloom. The stakes were higher than ever.

Her face flashed in my mind, the fear in her eyes

unsettling. What could I possibly offer her? I was a monster, cursed and hunted, not a savior. Still, the urge was undeniable, a magnetic pull that drew me closer to her.

Men scurried past, their laughter hollow against the market's vibrant backdrop. Their eyes darted around, alert and wary as if sensing the darkness that clung to me.

I tightened my grip on my jaw, feeling the shadows close in. The almost full moon loomed low in the sky, a relentless reminder of my curse, how I always remained in this form. Soon, the hunters would emerge, eager for a prize, and I was both their target and their fear. Wealth and status meant little to those who saw me as a rogue wolf, a danger to be eliminated.

I needed to get back to my home, back to safety. I hurried away, forcing myself to forget her, even as the image of her haunted me, a flicker of light in my otherwise dark existence.

$\mathcal{E}$mily

Night had fallen like a heavy velvet curtain, smothering the last blush of twilight. The cobble-stones beneath my feet, slick with a damp chill, mirrored the icy fear gripping my heart. Each echoing footfall was a painful reminder of the throbbing pain in my thigh, sending fresh waves of agony through me.

Lost and alone in this strange, shadowed city, I wrapped my arms around myself, the thin fabric of my T-shirt offering little comfort against the encroaching cold. I had no money, no friends, no sanctuary, only the gnawing fear in my gut that twisted tighter with every breath.

And then I remembered him—a werewolf. My mind scrambled, still struggling to believe it. How could it be? I had read about werewolves in my family's history research but had always dismissed them as mere folklore. Yet there he was, walking in a suit. This wasn't right. It felt like a nightmare from which I couldn't wake.

How could I get back home when I didn't even know how I had come to this place? I twirled the pendant in my fingers, wondering how it could send me home, but no light came from inside.

Desperation clawed at me. I needed to find shelter, a place to hide from the oppressive darkness that seemed to pulse with a life of its own.

My gaze darted from doorway to doorway, searching for an open window, a crack in a wall, anything that offered a sliver of refuge. But the tall and imposing buildings stood like silent, indifferent giants, their darkened windows staring back at me like empty eyes. Each breath caught in my chest, a strangled gasp against the rising tide of panic.

Turning a corner, hope flickered and died as I found myself trapped in a narrow, dead-end alley. The towering brick walls, slick with moss and grime, seemed to lean in, suffocating me. The air grew thick and heavy, pressing down on me with an almost physical weight. A shiver, colder than the night air, snaked down my spine.

And then I heard them. Not a sound, but a sensation, a chilling whisper that slithered through the darkness, wrapping around me like a silken noose. It was a voice of shadows, insidious and dark, promising oblivion.

My instincts screamed at me to run, to fight, but my limbs felt heavy, leaden with fear. It was too late.

They emerged from the depths of the alley, not men, not beasts, but a grotesque amalgamation of both, shadows given sinister form. Their edges twisted and writhed, coiling around me like a living nightmare, claw-like hands dripping with an unnatural darkness that glistened in the faint light.

As they closed in, an icy wave of dread washed over me, paralyzing my thoughts. I gasped, feeling my very essence being siphoned away as if they were draining me of everything that made me who I was. Panic surged within, igniting a desperate fight for survival. I clung fiercely to my memories, the warmth of my home, the laughter of friends, and the bright dreams that still flickered like distant stars. I wouldn't let them extinguish that light.

But their grip tightened, an iron vice around my spirit, and I felt myself slipping into the abyss. They were draining me, siphoning my life force, and each second felt like an eternity of pain.

Exhaustion crept in as I hugged myself tightly, as if my arms could shield me from the darkness. It was a battle against my fading will, more than against them.

As despair began to claw at my mind, a sudden force erupted from the shadows, scattering them like dry leaves in a tempest. I barely registered the figure that emerged—a tall, imposing man cloaked in darkness, yet somehow illuminated by the moon's pale light. His presence cast an ethereal glow, pushing back the encroaching shadows and igniting a flicker of hope within me.

"Get away from her!" His voice, a deep, resonant growl that reverberated through the narrow space, sliced through the oppressive silence. The shadows recoiled as if struck, hissing and spitting like enraged cats as they retreated into the night. The oppressive weight crushing me lifted, replaced by a dizzying lightness.

My vision swam, the alleyway shifting from a confining prison to a vast, empty expanse. Then I saw him. The image drawn by my father in his journal flashed in my mind. The mysterious NB was here in the flesh.

The moonlight caught the sharp angles of his

wolfish face. The elongated snout, the pointed ears, and the blazing amber eyes that burned into me with an unnerving intensity. His midnight-black fur shimmered with an unnatural luminescence, radiating a primal energy that both terrified and inexplicably drew me in.

He stood between the shadows and me, a formidable barrier. The raw, untamed power emanating from him was unsettling, a clear threat to anything that dared approach, and in that very danger, I found an undeniable assurance of protection. He was a wolf, the embodiment of lethal grace, yet his unwavering stance was a shield forged for me.

A whirlwind of emotions—fear, gratitude, disbelief—warred within me. He was a monster ripped from the darkest corners of my imagination, yet he had saved me.

My heart hammered against my ribs, a frantic rhythm against the sudden, unnerving quiet of the alley. The urge to run, to scream, was overwhelming, but a searing pain shot through my injured leg, anchoring me to the spot.

My gaze flicked back to the alley's mouth, the shadows writhed and coalesced, reforming into menacing shapes. Laced with malice, their silent whispers slithered back into my mind, icy tendrils of dread coiling around my heart.

He, this monstrous, terrifying being, was the only shield between the horrors that stalked him and me, the only sanctuary in this twisted, nightmarish reality. And in that agonizing moment, the paralyzing fear of the unknown was swallowed whole by the stark, visceral terror of what I knew. My fate, it seemed, was inextricably bound to this creature of darkness.

"I'm Lord Nathaniel Blackwood," he said, extending a hand, the gesture oddly formal amidst the chaos. "And you are?"

The absurdity of the situation and the polite introduction in the face of such monstrous horror almost made me laugh.

"Emily Warren," I managed, my voice trembling slightly.

His hand dropped, his gaze intensifying. "We can't stay here," he said, his voice low and urgent, a hint of desperation in his tone. "It's not safe. Come with me, Emily. I can help you."

I hesitated, caught in the crosscurrents of fear and the need to survive. The encroaching shadows seemed to press in on me, suffocating, waiting for him to go, and I knew I couldn't stay.

He was the NB my father had warned me about. Or had he been trying to *guide* me toward him? Could I trust him?

Doubt gnawed at me. He wasn't human, not entirely. He was something else, a creature of myth and legend, a beast, a monster. Yet, he was also the one offering me salvation.

But before I could move, a sudden cacophony shattered the silence, the unmistakable sound of footsteps pounding against the pavement.

"Stay right where you are!" a commanding voice boomed from the alley's entrance.

My heart raced as I turned to see figures emerging from the darkness, clad in rugged gear and armed with silver weapons glinting ominously in the moonlight. They were hunters, ruthless and relentless, their eyes locked onto Lord Nathaniel and me.

The air thickened with tension, and I felt the oppressive weight of dread settle over me once more. The hunters advanced, their expressions a mix of determination and malice.

I was trapped, caught between the dark promise of Nathaniel's protection and the lethal intent of the hunters.

Nathaniel growled, his body tense, ready to fight.

But I was frozen, my breath caught in my throat as the hunters closed in.

With the hunters closing in, I had to act fast. Would I trust the monster in front of me, or would I be left to the merciless fate that lay in wait?

38

CHAPTER 5

*L*ord Nathaniel Blackwood

Moonlight painted the alley in shades of silver and grime, glinting off the silver arrows pointed at me. Three hunters with grim faces blocked my escape, fear and loathing warred in their eyes.

"*Protecting* the lady, are we?" the tallest sneered, crossbow taut. "More like preyin' on her. She needs returnin' to the brothel." His gaze slid to Emily, cowering behind me. A low growl rumbled in my chest.

"She's been attacked," I snarled, my voice raw. "I'm protecting her." Emily trembled, her fear a living thing pressed against my back.

"Filthy beast," the stocky one spat.

My control fractured. They only saw the monster. Before they could advance, I lunged at the man closest to me, wrestling his arrow from his hand.

One of the men grabbed Emily, ripping her from my side, pulling her farther away from me. A primal roar tore from my throat. The separation was agony. How could this be?

I used the acquired arrow as my weapon, slashing at the men until it broke and I used my teeth and claws, flesh ripped, and the hot spray of blood splattered out. I fought with a desperate savagery but also with hate toward the hunters for attacking me. Each blow was a betrayal of the man I struggled to remain. What would she think, seeing my beast unleashed?

Then, a glimpse of Emily's face, pale but resolute. Our eyes met. Not fear, but understanding. It was enough.

With a final, desperate surge, I broke the face of the last man standing. He fell heavily to the ground. "Run!" I roared, turning toward her. Despite my fury, I hadn't killed any of them, even though a dark desire soared through me wanting to do so.

She hesitated, then nodded, running, no limping from the alley. Had she been hurt?

I followed, pain a searing brand in my side, but we needed to get away. If I killed the hunters, I would be in breach of further human laws set to contain me. I couldn't afford to allow that to happen.

We burst onto the street, the hunters' shouts echoing behind us. We ran, breath ragged, until a spied narrow side street offered refuge, and I pulled Emily toward it. Out of sight in a doorway, we caught our breaths.

Emily turned, her hand flying to her mouth as she saw my wounds. Crimson stained my fur, stark against the dark.

"You're hurt," she whispered, her voice trembling.

"It's nothing," I rasped, the lie a bitter taste. I didn't want her pity.

Her hand, tentative, brushed my fur. A jolt of electricity arced between us, melting the icy isolation with connection and understanding. A fragile ember of hope flickered in the darkness.

Footsteps echoed nearby. We had to move.

"I have to get home," I growled, the urgency clawing at me.

"How?" Fear edged her voice.

A carriage waited at the street's end. "There."

"Stay close," I commanded, my body screaming in protest with each step.

I hailed the carriage. "Get in," I told her, then barked orders to the driver on where to go.

Inside, the scent of leather and hay filled the air. Hooves drummed against cobblestones. Her gaze, heavy with concern, rested on me.

In the dim light of the carriage, something shifted between us. The fear in her eyes mingled with something else. Fascination?

Could she see past the monster to the man beneath? The terrifying and exhilarating thought held me captive as we rattled toward my home.

"Are you going to be okay?" she asked.

I grimaced, shrugging as if the pain were a mere annoyance. "I've had worse." The lie tasted like ash in my mouth. A throbbing ache pulsed through my side, a stark reminder of the shadows we'd barely escaped.

"Because you're a werewolf," she breathed out, her eyes wide with fear and fascination.

The scent of her perspiration, tinged with fear, filled the close confines of the carriage. I was a monster in her eyes. Any flicker of possibility between us, extinguished.

"Because I'm cursed," I corrected, the words raw.

"What?"

"The full moon…" I explained, my voice tight, "… is rising soon. This is when I should be changing.

Instead, I'm trapped. Part wolf, part man because of a curse from a witch."

"So… you're not the only… supernatural being?" She shifted. Her quickened pulse thrummed in the air.

"Werewolves, vampires, witches… they're not part of your everyday life?" I asked, watching her closely.

"No. Not in the future."

"Right. You're a time traveler like your father." I met her gaze, recognizing the same strength and stubborn set to her jaw. She'd had her world turned upside down, faced those shadows, and now me. "I can see the resemblance."

"You met him?"

"Once, briefly. Then he was gone." I hesitated. "He wasn't as… composed as you are."

"What do you mean?"

"Fear ruled him," I admitted, searching for the right words. "I saw him once, then… I assumed he returned to his own time."

"So, I can go back?" A flicker of hope in her voice.

"I imagine so," I said, my voice heavy. "But I don't know how."

The carriage rounded a corner too sharply, throwing Emily against me. Instinct took over. I caught her, her face inches from mine, hazel eyes locking with mine.

My pulse leaped. I lifted my paw, wanting to brush a stray auburn curl from her cheek, the thought of her skin against my claws both exhilarating and terrifying.

She leaned closer, her lips parted, and the urge to kiss her was a physical ache. But I couldn't. Not now. Not when she was still reeling from her journey through time.

Gently, I pushed her away, settling her beside me. A blush warmed her cheeks. Perhaps I should have kissed her anyway.

"I might be a monster..." I murmured, my voice rough, "... but I'm still a gentleman."

She nodded, her gaze fixed on her hands, lost in thoughts I longed to know.

"Why were you cursed?" she finally asked.

I sighed, the weight of the past settling on me. "Because I didn't follow the rules." I suppose it wouldn't hurt to tell her. "I come from a pure bloodline. One of wealth, respect, and responsibility."

"But..." She urged me to continue.

"Even so, we're expected to conform to human laws. On the full moon, we're confined, and if we can't control our... urges, we are locked away."

"And you couldn't?"

"Worse," I admitted, my voice heavy with the weight of the memory. "I went out and took my best mate, Alden Ashwood, with me. Young, stupid, and fueled by a reckless desire to rebel, I wanted to prove we could hunt under the full moon and that we didn't need these rules born of fear."

The pain of that night still burned within me. "I was nearly killed. Only lone wolves and rogues hunt under a full moon. Alden… he wasn't as lucky. My punishment, a curse, was inflicted by Isolde Thorne, who had served my family for decades." Bitterness laced my words, but beneath it lay the unshakeable truth. I deserved the curse. "Forever caught between wolf and man, unable to fully inhabit either world. A spell that could never be broken."

"And that's why you were hunted tonight."

"I shouldn't have gone out."

"Then why did you?"

For you. The words remained unspoken. I'd meant to ignore her and return to my home, but something had drawn me to linger, and then I found her.

The carriage bumped fast over the cobblestones, sending another jolt of pain through me. I gritted my teeth, fighting the fear that clawed at the edges of my control. Emily's gaze was on me, her compassion a tangible presence in the dim light.

"You protected me," she insisted, her voice unwavering. "You're not just a monster. You're a protector. You're still *you*."

I wanted to believe her. Beneath the curse, beneath the beast, I desperately wanted to believe there was still a man capable of love and protection. But the shadows of my past loomed, threatening to suffocate the fragile hope she had ignited.

The carriage jerked to a halt in front of my home. Alistair Finch, my loyal butler, had the door open before I could even reach for the handle.

"I'm fine," I muttered, waving him off. I didn't want a fuss. As I stepped down, I saw Alistair slip the driver a few extra notes. I could always count on him.

The carriage wheels crunched on the gravel driveway as it pulled away. The night's events finally caught up with me, and my legs gave way.

Emily was there in an instant, catching me before Alistair could react. He watched us, a flicker of concern quickly replaced by curiosity. I hadn't brought a woman home since being cursed. This wasn't like that, though I knew my servants—eager for me, the last of my line to marry—would hope otherwise.

"Meet Emily," I said to Alistair, my voice strained.

"She'll be staying for a bit. Have Nora wake the cook and prepare the guest room."

"A pleasure to meet you, Miss," Alistair said, his voice smooth and professional.

"Emily, this is Alistair," I managed. "If you need anything, ask him."

Then my vision blurred. Voices raised in alarm and color swirled around me, but I couldn't focus. For a moment, I saw Emily's face in the encroaching darkness before I lost consciousness.

$\mathscr{E}$mily

Nathaniel's room wasn't merely elegant, it was a masterpiece of shadowed opulence. Deep hues of velvet and silk drank the candlelight, while the gazes of ancestral portraits, frozen in oils, felt curious and accusatory. The scent of aged leather and polished wood, a subtle echo of Nathaniel, wrapped around me, a comforting yet alien embrace. I was an intruder in this world, a ghost haunting the edges of a life I didn't understand.

Having retreated from the bedside while Alistair ministered to Nathaniel, I paced the plush carpet, a restless energy thrumming beneath my skin.

Without the medical developments that we had in the future, I couldn't see how he would survive. And that worried me sick. He was, after all, the only creature—*beast?*—who had shown me a flicker of compassion since the shadows of time had swallowed me whole. The exhaustion from their relentless feeding still clung to me, a chilling weight in my soul.

"Lord Blackwood," Alistair's clipped voice cut through the silence. "Your wounds require attention."

"I'm fine, Alistair," Nathaniel's strained but resolute voice came from the bed. "We're safe here."

"Safe, perhaps…" the butler retorted, his tone laced with disapproval, "… but reckless. Have you not learned your lesson? Perhaps Isolde's curse was a necessary evil."

Nathaniel's silence was a tacit admission of guilt. I moved closer to the bed, drawn by an inexplicable need to bridge the distance between us.

"He's right, you know," I said softly, perching on the edge of the bed. "Let me help." My gaze met Nathaniel's with a silent plea for understanding.

"It won't take long," I added, hoping to ease the tension.

A flicker of something unreadable crossed Nathaniel's face before he relented with a grimace.

He sat up, the movement revealing the extent of his injuries. As he shed his waistcoat and shirt, my breath hitched, not at the sight of blood, but at the sight of him—toned muscles, corded with power, stretched beneath a coat of dark, inviting fur.

My fingers tingled, aching to trace the lines of his body, to feel the warmth beneath the fur. The beast, so recently unleashed, now lay vulnerable before me, and the urge to touch him, to offer comfort, was almost overwhelming.

Alistair moved with practiced efficiency, his touch gentle yet firm as he cleansed Nathaniel's wounds. He shaved the fur back away from the wounds before cleansing the area.

"This is a new technique," he said proudly to me as the sharp tang of pure ethanol filled the air, starkly contrasting the lingering scent of leather and wood. I had to remind myself that everything I knew and used hadn't been invented or discovered yet.

I watched, mesmerized, as the now cleaned crimson gashes began to close before my eyes, the torn flesh knitting itself back together with unnatural speed. A gasp escaped my lips.

"The transformation…" Nathaniel murmured, his voice a low rumble, "… accelerated healing. A blessing and a curse."

"Indeed," Alistair added, his tone dry as he

disposed of the bloodied bandages. "Though cleanliness never goes amiss, even for a werewolf." His lips twitched in a rare smile, a brief flicker of warmth in his otherwise stoic demeanor.

The weariness clinging to me intensified, a bone-deep ache that mirrored the longing in my heart. The desire to be close to Nathaniel, to wrap myself in the warmth of his fur, to feel the steady beat of his heart against mine, was becoming almost unbearable. Alistair's presence was the only thing holding me back. Once he left, I knew my resolve would crumble.

Just as I thought I could bear it no longer, even with Alistair still in the room, a soft knock announced the arrival of Nora, a young maid carrying a tray laden with steaming bowls of chicken soup.

"From Cook," she announced, her voice bright. "And a message. This is his last meal if he ever pulls a stunt like that again on a full moon."

A chuckle escaped Nathaniel, a low rumble in his chest. "My servants are nothing if not consistent," he said, his gaze meeting mine with a spark of amusement that sent a wave of heat through me. The intensity of his stare, the raw power that emanated from him, ignited a fresh wave of desire, a yearning that went far beyond the physical.

"Is there anything else, my Lord?" asked Alistair.

"No, thank you," responded Nathaniel. Alistair bowed and slipped from the room.

Nathaniel made to stand, but Nora, ever attentive, gently pressed him back down. "Easy, my Lord," she chided, her tone laced with genuine concern. "Based on the condition of your shirt and the sheets, clearly you've lost a lot of blood."

I took a bowl of soup and settled at his feet on the bed, the warmth of the broth a welcome comfort. The closeness, even this small gesture of intimacy, sent a thrill through me.

After ensuring we were settled, Nora gave a small curtsy. "I'll return shortly for the bowls," she said, her gaze lingering on me for a moment. "And then, Miss Emily, I'll draw you a hot bath. I'm sure you could use one." With another smile, she slipped out of the room, leaving us alone in the soft glow of the candlelight.

A hot bath sounded like a comfort I could lose myself in. Except I was almost lost in his eyes, alone with him in his bedroom.

The rhythmic clinking of spoons against china was a soothing counterpoint to the frantic beat of my heart. The rich broth warmed me from the inside out, chasing away the lingering chill of fear and exhaustion. The crusty bread, still warm from the oven, was a welcome sustenance. The meal was the distraction I needed to stop me from acting on my desires, but I couldn't find my voice.

I savored the last bite, a question bubbled to the surface that I had been contemplating during the meal. "The shadows…" I began, my voice hesitant, "… the creatures in the alley… what were they?"

Nathaniel's gaze darkened, a flicker of unease crossing his features. He set his spoon down, the quiet click echoing in the sudden stillness. "They are drawn to unusual energies," he explained, his voice low and measured. "Like the energy surrounding you, a residue of your… journey through time."

So, my arrival in this time wasn't just a random occurrence for the shadows to seek me out. It had made me a target.

"They're vampiric…" he continued, his gaze fixed on mine, "… in their need to feed off energy. But they're not true vampires. They're controlled and are minions of a greater power." He paused, his jaw tightening. "And that's what worries me. I don't know who, or what, is controlling them."

"And they targeted me?" A shiver ran down my spine. The idea of being hunted by creatures controlled by an unknown entity was terrifying.

"Yes, they were certainly homing in on the

energy that surrounded you from time traveling and then started draining you."

"And my father?" I asked, the words barely a whisper. This had to do with my father, right? "Did they feed on him too?"

Nathaniel hesitated, his expression unreadable. "I don't know," he finally admitted, his voice heavy with regret. "I saw him only briefly. He was… frightened and disoriented. And then he was gone." He reached across the small space separating us, his paw covering mine in a gesture of comfort. The warmth of his touch and the tickle of his fur sent a jolt of electricity through me with a strange mix of fear and reassurance.

The shadows probably had fed on him. I shuddered thinking of what I might be like now if Nathaniel hadn't come along when he did.

But then another thought came to mind. "Or maybe my father knew who was controlling them."

"That would give him cause to be fearful."

"And now I'm here…" My mouth dried, and the words caught in my throat.

"You have survived a feeding, which tells me you are very strong. And you have something else." His paw on my arm gave me the strength I needed, but it also flamed the desire to lie next to him and move my hands over his furred body.

"What?" I asked.

"Me to protect you."

My eyes met his, and I knew my resolve was gone. Any doubt whether I should do this or not was gone. If he hadn't been such a gentleman, I might not feel this way, but beast or not, I wanted him.

He leaned toward me, and I responded, but then a sharp knock at the door sent us pulling away, and my mind reeled back to reality.

I had shadows coming after me.

"Miss, your bath is ready."

"Go." Gestured Nathaniel as if he could sense I didn't want to leave him. "Rest, and tomorrow we can continue our discussions."

"Goodnight, Lord Blackwood," I said, standing from the bed, handing my bowl to Nora.

"Call me Nathaniel, please."

"Goodnight, Nathaniel." His name felt like velvet on my lips. Then I followed Nora, ever so reluctantly from his room, wishing I were spending the night next to him.

mily

The water, almost too hot, initially stung my skin, then settled into a soothing warmth that eased the knot in my shoulders, back, and legs. The horse hoof left a dreadful black bruise on my leg, but thank goodness, no broken bones. I couldn't heal like Nathaniel.

Steam curled around me, blurring the edges of the guest bedroom, transforming it into a hazy sanctuary. I sank deeper into the copper tub, letting the water lap against my chin, trying to wash away the night's lingering unease.

The pendant, still around my neck, seemed to

pulse with faint energy. Had my father truly been crazy, or had he simply seen too much, lost too much energy to the shadows?

I closed my eyes, trying to push away the rising tide of anxiety. I needed to focus, to think clearly. What was the Moonlight Promenade? What did my father want me to find? The questions swirled in my mind, unanswered, like the steam rising from the water.

My thoughts drifted to Nathaniel, his image flickering behind my closed eyelids. The way he'd looked at me, the intensity in his eyes, the raw power he held barely in check both thrilled and terrified me.

The memory of his touch, the brief brush of his paw against my hand, sent a shiver down my spine, a strange mix of fear and longing.

The water, still warm against my skin, seemed to amplify the heat blooming within me as my thoughts drifted to Nathaniel. I pictured him shirtless, the moonlight catching the subtle ripples of his fur, a captivating blend of power and vulnerability.

A thrill, sharp and unexpected, shot through me. I imagined the texture of that fur beneath my fingertips, the surprising softness, the way it might ripple beneath my touch. The image of his teeth, sharp yet elegant, sent a shiver down my spine. What would it be like to feel those teeth against my lips, not in a threatening way, but in a kiss?

The thought, forbidden and exhilarating, ignited a fire within me, a heat that settled deep in my core. Closing my eyes, I surrendered to the fantasy, the warmth of the water amplifying the burgeoning desire, pulling me into a swirling vortex of sensation. My breath hitched, a soft moan escaping my lips as the daydream intensified, Nathaniel's image vivid in my mind. The steamy haze of the bath blurred the line between reality and imagination, my skin tingling with anticipation.

My fingers drifted down my belly, slipping into the intimate folds between my legs, the touch sending a ripple of longing through me. The question, unspoken yet burning, echoed in my mind. What would it feel like to have his paws touching me there? The thought alone sent a tremor through my body, a deep ache of wanting. I yearned, with a sudden, desperate intensity, to know.

A soft knock at the door startled me. "Miss Emily? Are you all right? Do you need anything?" Nora's voice, muffled through the thick wooden door, broke through my sexy adult time.

My eyes flew open. Mortified, I realized I'd been lost in thought, completely unaware of the passing time. I quickly sat up in the now lukewarm water, grabbing the thick, lush white towel to cover myself. A screen between the bath and the bed gave me privacy, but still, I wasn't used to such attention.

"I'm fine, Nora," I called out, my voice slightly shaky. "Just enjoying the bath."

"Very good, Miss. I have a nightgown for you. A fine cambric one, trimmed with Valenciennes lace and embroidered with silk floss roses. Shall I come in and assist you from the bath?"

The description of the nightgown made me blush further. It sounded far too luxurious for someone like me. But worse, the idea of being assisted from the copper tub sent me splashing to get out and covering myself with the towel.

"No, thank you, Nora. I can manage."

She flung the nightgown over the top of the screen and left it hanging there for me. I could hear Nora moving on the other side of the screen, preparing the bed, and I breathed a sigh of relief that she wasn't persistent about helping me. Though I thought cheekily, if it were Nathaniel asking, I would let him.

The nightgown, as described, was indeed exquisite. The fine cambric felt cool and smooth against my skin, and the delicate lace and embroidery were breathtaking. It was a far cry from my simple cotton shorts and tank top I wore to bed back in my own time, and I felt a strange mix of guilt and pleasure wearing something so fine.

I emerged from behind the dressing screen to find Nora placing a pan between the sheets. "To warm the sheets for you, Miss," she explained.

God a girl could get used to this luxury. I moved hesitantly toward the large, canopied bed, the luxurious linens adding to the surreal feeling of the evening. Had time travel inadvertently made me win some sort of historical lottery?

"Is Nathaniel married?" I blurted out, the question escaping before I could stop it.

"No, Miss," Nora replied, shaking her head. "We've been encouraging him to find a wife for a long time, but he won't have it."

"Why?"

"On account of the curse, Miss. He believes no woman would want him."

I would want him. Right here, right now. The thought shocked me with its intensity, but it was undeniably true. I'd always been adventurous, open to new experiences.

"Does the curse stop him…" I trailed off, unsure how to phrase the delicate question.

"He can have children, Miss. Or wolflings, I suppose," Nora answered, her tone matter-of-fact.

"I mean… this," I gestured vaguely around the

opulent room, my cheeks burning. Nora had inadvertently answered a question lingering in my mind, one I hadn't quite dared to voice.

"Oh, you mean his position in human society?" Nora clarified, her expression understanding.

"Yes, can he maintain this wealth despite… everything?"

"It's because of the Blackwood bloodline, Miss. Old money, passed down through generations."

Of course. He was the mysterious NB, the initials matching the sketch in my father's journal. But in my own time, he'd been a significant benefactor to the university, though there was no documentation to suggest he was a werewolf. Did that philanthropy mean he wouldn't have children, wolflings, or otherwise? The question tugged at me, a strange tightness in my chest. Why did the thought of him being alone, without heirs, cause me such a pang?

"But werewolves live amongst humans?" I asked, still trying to reconcile the pieces of this strange society in a past I knew nothing about.

"Humans are the rulers, Miss, but yes," Nora replied. "And before you get too wound up, I'm human myself. Not all the staff are, though. There's a fae, a witch, and other werewolves, but no vampires," she added with a reassuring smile.

"Oh…" I sighed, taking it all in.

"No need to be scared, Miss. Come on, into bed with you." She removed the warming pan from between the sheets.

I followed her advice, sliding between the luxurious linens. My feet found the deliciously warm spot, a small comfort amid this overwhelming strangeness.

"You'll be safe with him. Don't worry, he'll look after you. Now, you'd better get some rest. I can't believe you're still awake," Nora said, her voice gentle.

Then she left, the door clicking softly shut behind her. I was alone in the enormous bed, cocooned in warmth and softness, but sleep remained elusive. I had traveled back in time, narrowly escaped death, and was now harboring inappropriate thoughts about a werewolf. Just as I was drifting toward unconsciousness, a low growl resonated from the other side of the door, a sound that was both unsettling and strangely alluring.

Dare I call out? Then I heard footsteps going away, my chance to call him into my room was gone.

CHAPTER 8

*L*ord Nathaniel Blackwood

I couldn't resist the pull. Despite the gnawing need for rest and the even stronger need to keep my distance, I had to go to her room. Every moment spent in her presence chipped away at my control and fueled the dangerous desires simmering beneath the surface.

The long hallway stretched before me, and moonlight filtered through the arched windows, casting elongated shadows that danced with the flickering candle flames in their sconces. The scent of lavender and beeswax hung in the air, a stark contrast to the primal, earthy scent that clung to me, a constant reminder of what I was. My footsteps were silent on the thick carpet as I approached her door, each step a battle against the urge to turn back, to protect her from the beast within me.

I could smell her, sweet and intoxicating, a delicate floral fragrance that mingled with her pheromones. I could hear the steady rhythm of her heartbeat, a soothing counterpoint to the turbulent storm raging within my chest.

I heard her shift in the bed, the rustle of the sheets a torment against my strained senses. Then, with a groan of frustration, I turned and fled, retreating to the sanctuary of my room before I disgraced myself by entering hers and taking what I craved, what I knew I shouldn't. Could I be certain she was willing? I was neither man nor beast, a creature trapped between two worlds, forever caught in the agonizing chasm between desire and restraint.

My room, vast and shadowed, offered little solace. The heavy velvet curtains were drawn, shrouding the space in an almost suffocating darkness. Moonlight barely penetrated the gloom, reflecting dully off the polished mahogany furniture and the silver-framed portraits of my ancestors that lined the walls, their gazes seeming to follow me, judging my every move. Sleep came in fitful bursts, tormented by fragmented memories of the past.

Something elusive danced just beyond my grasp, a vital clue hidden within the labyrinth of my memories. Whenever I came close, I was pulled away, yanked back to the starting point of my endless search.

How had she traveled back to this time? And why? I suspected a hereditary component, mirroring her father's journey, but there had to be other triggers, other methods to initiate such a temporal shift. I needed to know.

But even more pressing was the mystery of who controlled the shadows. This was the true threat, the danger that loomed over her. While humans held the reins of power, families like mine maintained a precarious balance, preventing the eruption of chaos within the hidden world.

My curse, however, hampered my efforts, isolating me, leaving me the last of my line. In sleep, the answer remained just out of reach. Awake, my mind raced, sifting through a list of potential adversaries, none of whom seemed powerful enough to wield such dark magic.

The pre-dawn chill clung to the air as I rose from my bed, the lingering remnants of a restless sleep clinging to me like cobwebs. I crossed the room, the floorboards creaking softly beneath my bare feet, and lit a single candle on my desk.

The flickering flame cast long, dancing shadows across the walls, illuminating the scattered papers and open books. I picked up a quill and dipped it in ink, the scratching sound oddly loud in the room's stillness.

On a fresh sheet of parchment, I carefully inscribed four names—Lady Seraphina Voss, her reputation for dark sorcery preceding her, Reginald of the Darkwood Clan, the ruthless alpha of a rogue werewolf pack, The Whispering Witch, a shadowy figure spoken of in hushed tones, and Alaric the Alchemist, whose obsession with forbidden knowledge was legendary.

Each name represented a potential threat, a possible key to the mystery surrounding the shadows. With a sigh, I set the quill down, the weight of responsibility settling heavily upon my shoulders. I extinguished the candle and left the room, the faint scents of ink, parchment, and smoke lingering in the air.

A sliver of anticipation warmed me as I descended the stairs toward the dining room, the prospect of Emily's company a welcome distraction from the darkness that threatened to consume me. Had she slept well? It warmed me to know that she had slept in my house, though I'd much prefer it if it had been in my bed.

I sat at the long, polished table, the morning light spilling through the windows, illuminating the lavish breakfast spread. My thoughts were miles away when a soft rustle, like the whisper of secrets, drew my attention. Emily stood in the doorway, and my breath caught. My pulse, previously calm, became a frantic drum against my ribs.

The gown she wore was a revelation. A deep, sapphire blue, it clung to her curves like a second skin, the rich fabric molding to the swell of her breasts, the nip of her waist, and the gentle flare of her hips. The daringly low neckline revealed a tantalizing glimpse of creamy skin and the delicate hollow of her throat. It was a dress designed to entice, to inflame, and it succeeded admirably. A possessive heat, a primal urge to claim her, surged through me.

She smiled shyly, a soft "Good morning" escaping her lips, and glided toward the table.

I watched, captivated, as she filled her plate, her movements imbued with an unconscious sensuality. Then, with a delightful disregard for convention, she ignored the place setting prepared for her and chose the seat beside me. The subtle act of rebellion and the quiet defiance of societal expectations sent a thrill through me. A low chuckle, a rumble of pure, masculine appreciation, vibrated in my chest.

"How are you feeling this morning?" Emily asked, her voice barely above a whisper, her gaze searching mine.

Like I want to devour you, I thought, the primal urge a fierce, almost painful ache. I forced a smile, a poor imitation of composure.

"All healed," I replied, the lie a bitter taste on my tongue. "And you? Did you sleep well?"

"I did, though I felt lost in such a big bed," she admitted, a hint of vulnerability in her voice that sent a protective surge through me.

A low, involuntary growl rumbled in my chest, a response to her unspoken need I desperately wanted to fulfill. *Focus, Nathaniel.* I had to keep my distance and maintain some semblance of control.

"Have you had any thoughts on how you managed to arrive in this time?" I asked, forcing myself to focus on the practical, the logical.

"I'm not entirely sure," she said, her fingers toying with the pendant's chain, drawing my attention to the delicate hollow of her throat. "But I believe it has something to do with this."

With a deep breath, she pulled the pendant from beneath her gown, the silver glinting in the morning light. My gaze lingered, for a heartbeat too long, on the soft swell of her breasts, barely concealed by the fabric, before I forced myself to focus on the artifact.

"It belonged to my father," she continued, her voice trembling slightly. "He sent it to me after his death… almost as if he knew this would happen. As if he planned it all before he… before he passed away."

"I'm sorry," I whispered, the words inadequate, a hollow echo of the empathy I felt. "He didn't deserve his life to end that way."

She nodded, her eyes glistening with unshed tears, and picked up a cup of tea, taking a small, shaky sip. The urge to reach out, to pull her close and offer comfort, was almost overwhelming.

"May I see the pendant?" I extended my paw, the request a deliberate attempt to break the spell and regain some semblance of control.

She placed the pendant in my outstretched paw, her fingers brushing against my fur, the simple act surprisingly intimate, a silent exchange of vulnerability. The coolness of the metal against my skin was a jarring contrast to the sudden, intense heat that flared within me. *Damn it, Nathaniel. Focus.*

I examined the intricate design, forcing myself to concentrate on the details. The symbol was undeniably familiar, a chilling echo of the tattoos I'd seen on the wolf hunters who had attacked us the previous night. My blood ran cold, a wave of unease washing over me.

What possible connection could this woman, this innocent stranger, have with those ruthless mercenaries? Everything I thought I knew suddenly felt uncertain, precarious. I looked up at Emily, my gaze searching, probing.

"Tell me, Emily…" I said, my voice strained, "…what do you know about this symbol?"

"The same symbol was in my father's journal," she explained, her voice hesitant. "He wrote about it being a symbol of the wolf hunters." She looked at me, her eyes widening with a dawning horror. "The men… they had it tattooed on them last night. I'm sorry… does it mean they're my ancestors?"

"I doubt any of them were," I said, trying to reassure her, but a knot of unease tightened in my gut. "But it's possible you are of wolf hunter heritage." The words hung in the air between us, a heavy, unspoken threat. *Her kind hunted my kind.* The thought was a cold, hard barrier, a seemingly insurmountable obstacle.

"I would never hurt you, Nathaniel."

Her words, spoken with such fierce conviction, sent a jolt of something akin to hope through me. But could I trust her? Could I trust my instincts and desires? I was falling for her, fast and hard, and the potential for heartbreak and betrayal was a terrifying prospect.

"I'm not the product of my ancestors. Just because they hunted your kind, I wouldn't."

"I can say some werewolves out there should be hunted." My words didn't come out as lighthearted as I had hoped.

"I don't believe that."

"I suppose that's why humans have the rule that no werewolves are to be out on a full moon, because in the past, there were those who couldn't control the change and went on a killing rampage."

"Does this happen now?"

"No, we train to control the transformation."

"Time for a change to this rule." She reached over and put her hand on my paw, her heat sending my pulse racing. "But what would these hunters need to time travel for?"

"I don't know." It was annoying because I was well-read and knew most things. "But your perspective is progressive, and I doubt they would have planned that to be the case."

"And my father made sure I had the pendant. What if there were others on the same lineage he could've given it to but didn't?" She took a deep breath. "You know the night I received this, I thought I saw a wolf standing outside."

"That's not good, you're in more danger than you think," I said hurriedly. I had to protect her.

"What if they were here to get it, but I got it."

"And why would your dad want you to get this pendant. He would've kept you safe by not giving it to you and destroying it."

Her eyes went watery. "Because he knew that I wouldn't hunt werewolves. I would do the opposite and advocate for them."

"But you had no idea that I am worthy of this."

"You are, I know in my time there's a legacy you left from the money you gave the university where I study."

"Really?" I liked the sound of that.

"So maybe he wants me to stop something."

"The problem is, I don't believe the hunters were controlling the shadows," I said.

"Which means there's another player in this… game."

"Exactly." I couldn't believe how logical and intelligent Emily was. The attraction to her flared, even though she had a pendant of my enemies.

"Who?"

"No idea." I shook my head. "But first, how exactly did the pendant pull you back in time? You are touching it now, but nothing is happening. So there's more to its power."

"I recited these words…"

"Hush!" I interrupted, my voice sharp. "Don't say them here. Not now."

Confusion clouded Emily's features. "Why?"

"We don't know what they might do," I explained, my tone softer now but still laced with caution. "It could be dangerous."

"Dangerous?" Emily echoed. "You mean… they could send me back?" A hint of longing colored her voice, a longing I couldn't quite decipher.

I studied her face, searching for an answer to a question I didn't want to voice. "Do you *want* to go back?"

"I…" Emily hesitated, her gaze dropping to the pendant still clutched in my hand. "I suppose so."

The words were barely audible, tinged with a disappointment that mirrored my own, though for vastly different reasons.

I tightened my grip on the pendant. "I believe this symbol is part of your heritage. Wolf hunters. It's in your blood. That, combined with the words, activated the pendant."

"But I didn't *intend* to come here," Emily protested, her voice rising in frustration. "I had no control over it."

"Perhaps some of the necessary steps were lost over time," I mused, my mind racing to put the possibilities together that fit the best. "But you clearly retained enough knowledge to activate the pendant and arrive here, just as your father did before you. Maybe… maybe you *should* go back, Emily. It would be safer."

"No!" Her response was immediate, emphatic. The single word vibrated with unexpected strength, a determination that surprised me.

"But your kind hunted mine. They killed my kind."

Emily's eyes met mine, unwavering. "I am not my ancestors," she stated firmly. "I would never hurt you. And I will *not* align myself with those… those hunters."

I searched her face, trying to gauge her sincerity. "Then why are you here, Emily?" I asked, my voice barely a whisper.

She hesitated, her gaze distant as if searching for an answer in the swirling mists of her confusion. "To right the wrongs of the past. To put a stop to the killing. Because my father believed in me to do it."

"I wish it were that simple." I sighed, the weight of centuries of conflict pressing down on me.

"But you won't know unless you try," Emily countered, her voice quiet but firm. Her unwavering optimism, so at odds with the grim reality of our situation, was both unsettling and strangely compelling.

I gave a wry chuckle. "True."

I picked at the food on my plate, trying to keep my paws busy so I didn't reach across the table and touch her, to feel the warmth of her skin against me.

I could almost taste the sweet scent of her desire, her pheromones swirling around me, intoxicating and distracting. I needed air, space, a reprieve from the intensity growing between us.

I abruptly pushed away from the table, the chair legs scraping against the floor with a jarring screech. "There's only one thing for it," I said.

"What?" Emily whispered, her eyes wide with a mixture of anticipation and apprehension.

"A walk," I declared, turning toward the door. "A walk in nature. Or at least, the closest approximation we can manage here in London." I paused. "Unless you have a better idea."

For a moment, she looked utterly bewildered, and the sight sent a surprising warmth through me. Then, her expression cleared, replaced by a decisive look that quickened my pulse.

"Let's go then. We have some serious theories to come up with on how best to stop the hunters and whoever is controlling the shadows." She rose gracefully, her perfume lingering in the air as she left her breakfast uneaten.

Then she paused. "Are you sure? What will people think when they see me?"

"Isn't he a lucky gentleman to have such a beautiful woman to stroll with?" I enjoyed the flush in her cheeks and the sound of her giggle. Even with the seriousness of our situation, I couldn't resist the urge to turn heads and fuel the gossip mill.

          *E*mily

Sunlight, dappled and warm, filtered through the leaves of ancient oaks, painting the path ahead in shifting patterns of light and shadow. The air hung heavily with the perfume of roses, a scent so intense it almost overpowered Nathaniel's hint of spicy wolf as we strolled through the gardens. I didn't think much of the dress Nora had helped me into—tight bodice, low cut, and yards and yards of silky soft blue hung around my legs.

Clearly, this was the thing to do in the mornings as many couples and groups of people were here, walking around, pausing to have whispered conversations. But this was nothing like I had ever experienced because not everyone here was human.

A flash of iridescent blue caught my eye—a pair of fae, their gossamer wings scattering sunlight as they walked past a bed of vibrant lilies. A small, hunched figure with pointed ears scuttled past, dressed in a tailored suit and waistcoat. A goblin, perhaps?

Further down the path, two figures strolled arm in arm, their laughter echoing through the gardens. One, a woman with flowing auburn hair, moved with an ethereal grace that seemed to defy gravity. The other, tall and imposing, with skin the color of polished bronze and eyes like chips of obsidian, walked with a quiet confidence that commanded attention.

My mind reeled, struggling to reconcile the streets I was used to. Where I'd been in the 21st century with its Wi-Fi and distinct lack of mythical beings felt like a distant dream.

Beside me, Nathaniel radiated an unconscious power that commanded attention. He navigated the bustling pathways of Regent's Park with an almost languid ease, a stark contrast to the turmoil I felt churning within me. I observed the subtle rituals of his world of rustling silks, whispered conversations, top hats, and parasols. It was a grandeur I'd only ever glimpsed in period dramas, where social status was everything, and a single misstep could ruin a reputation.

As we passed a group of elegantly dressed women, their laughter echoing like wind chimes in the crisp air, one of them, a woman in a striking emerald green gown, dipped into a low curtsy.

"Lord Blackwood," a woman's voice purred, cutting through the gentle murmur of the park. Her eyes, the color of molten gold, flickered over Nathaniel with a knowing smile. "How lovely to see you. And who is this enchanting creature gracing your arm?" Like heat rising from the pavement, a faint shimmer danced around her fingertips before dissipating into the air. Was that magic?

Nathaniel inclined his head, his expression giving nothing away. "Lady Beatrice. Emily, Lady Beatrice."

"A pleasure," Lady Beatrice murmured, her gaze lingering on Nathaniel a beat too long. "I trust I'll see you at the Summer Solstice gathering?"

"Perhaps," Nathaniel replied, his voice cool and noncommittal.

Lady Beatrice's smile didn't falter, but a subtle shift in her eyes hinted at a flicker of annoyance. "You must come, and I expect to see you, Emily." With a graceful nod, she continued down the path, her companions trailing behind her like shadows.

The air crackled faintly in her wake, a subtle scent of ozone lingering.

I glanced at Nathaniel, curious about the exchange. "The Summer Solstice gathering?"

He shrugged, his gaze meeting mine for a fleeting moment before drifting back to the path ahead. "A social event, more for witches." His tone was dismissive.

I suddenly had an interest in everyone around us —if they were human or not and what their social standings were.

"And what about that man over there?" I asked, nodding to a businessman who approached us, his eyes bright with ambition.

"Ah, Mr. Hargrove," Nathaniel said, his tone shifting slightly. "He's been trying to secure my endorsement for his new shipping line. A smart man, but he's a little too eager for my taste."

"Lord Blackwood, I was hoping to catch you. Would you do me the honor of joining me for dinner next Saturday? I believe we could discuss some exciting opportunities," he said, a forced smile stretched across his face.

Nathaniel's demeanor remained calm, but I felt his body tense. "I'll consider it, Mr. Hargrove. Until then."

The businessman nodded, visibly intimidated,

before backing away, casting furtive glances over his shoulder as if Nathaniel's presence was too powerful to linger around for long.

"You certainly know everyone," I remarked, my voice tinged with admiration and a touch of unease as we continued walking. It was exhilarating and slightly terrifying to be privy to these whispered secrets.

"I make it my business," Nathaniel said, his voice turning serious, the playful glint in his eyes replaced by a steely resolve. "It's the best way to protect myself. With the… curse…" he hesitated, the word hanging heavy in the air between us, "… and the ever-present threat of wolf hunters, I need to know who my allies and enemies are. I can't afford to be caught off-guard as I'm always on the back foot."

He paused, his gaze sweeping across the park, a flicker of frustration crossing his features. "Which is why it's so infuriating that I can't identify who's controlling the shadows."

"Why would anyone want to control them?" I questioned, even now, I didn't feel like my full energetic self since the attack.

"Normally, they are solitary creatures preying on fear and vulnerability, perhaps taking the odd life here and there, but I've never heard of them working together as a pack. It certainly makes them a weapon that's hard to track. Making this even more mysterious."

Nathaniel stopped dead in his tracks, his hand brushing against mine as he turned. An unexpected and electric jolt shot up my arm, leaving a trail of warmth in its wake. My heart pounded against my ribs, a frantic drumbeat against the sudden hush that fell between us. The bustling park faded away, and the sounds of laughter and distant carriage wheels were swallowed by the charged silence.

His eyes, alight with a sudden intensity, met mine. For a heartbeat, the world held its breath, leaving only the two of us suspended in a space filled with unspoken longing. The air thrummed with an energy I couldn't name, a strange mix of excitement and apprehension that made my breath catch in my throat.

His touch... I realized with a start but couldn't finish.

"That's it," he breathed, his voice a low rumble that sent shivers down my spine. "Whoever is controlling the shadows is looking for time travelers." His fingers, warm and strong, tightened around mine for a fleeting moment before he released me, the touch lingering like a phantom sensation on my skin. "They knew you didn't belong here," he added, his gaze searching my face as if seeking reassurance or perhaps something more.

"But why?" I whispered, my voice barely audible above the sudden pounding of my heart.

His jaw tightened almost imperceptibly. "I'm not sure," he murmured, his hand instinctively moving toward his coat pocket. "We should get back to my home. I need to review my notes."

At that moment, a figure darted past us, a fleeting shadow against the vibrant backdrop of the gardens. I barely registered their presence, just a flicker of movement at the edge of my vision, but Nathaniel stiffened, his whole body tensed like a coiled spring.

He unfolded a small parchment, fitting in his paw, moving his shoulder so I couldn't read it, then scrunched it up in his fist. A dark storm brewed in his eyes, and angry heat radiated from him.

"Who was the note from?" I asked, my voice shaky. My stomach knotted, and I placed my hand on my belly, finding it harder to breathe.

"No one," he responded sharply.

"And the note? What did it say?" It may have been delivered by 'no one,' but the way he had changed instantly had my heart palpitating and wishing we hadn't left his home.

CHAPTER 10

*L*ord Nathaniel Blackwood

I moved closer to her.

I scanned everyone around us, calculating whether they were a threat. The crumpled note burned against my paw, a physical manifestation of the threat it contained.

Hand her over. It's for her own good.

The words, scrawled in hurried ink, were haunting, sending my fur standing on end. Was this due to time travel and the shadows or something else?

And it was causing Emily to be on edge. I could smell her fear, hear her increased heartbeat, and feel the tension as she walked by my side. I had been a fool to bring her here in public. I had only been thinking of how a walk would help us come closer to learning what was going on, a walk was always something that helped me, and since it was daytime, I wagered the shadows wouldn't be a problem. How wrong could I be?

How could I have exposed her to my darkness, this world of whispered threats I lived in? My protective instincts roared to life, battling the chilling implications of the note. No way would I hand her over. This had to be a carefully laid trap, a ploy to separate us, to isolate me and exploit my vulnerability?

"Nathaniel." Her voice broke through the war of thoughts in my mind with a gentleness that touched my soul. "What is going on?"

I couldn't tell her, I couldn't admit that I only had theories.

"Emily," I began, my voice strained, the casual tone a thin veneer over the fear clawing at my throat. "Come, we don't want to stay out and get too much sun."

Her brow furrowed slightly. "Don't lie to me."

I increased my pace, forcing her to keep up. I had to get her out of here.

"Nathaniel." She stopped walking. "I'm not moving until you tell me."

I sighed and turned back to her. "Emily… there's no time…" I stopped inches from her, my heart suddenly hammering for me to kiss her lips.

I swallowed hard. "I just got a note."

"What did it say?" Her tone was commanding, which turned me on. Women never spoke to me like that, but I also didn't want to alarm her.

"Whatever it was, just tell me. I've traveled through time. Keeping it from me is only going to make things worse."

She had a point. But I wasn't used to being so open and honest.

"I don't want you to worry." I managed to say.

"I am worrying."

"Then stop," I said.

"Show me the note, Nathaniel." Her eyes, usually sparkling with amusement, were now dark with fear and suspicion. "Or I'll go ask Lady Beatrice for help."

The mere mention of Lady Beatrice's name sent a jolt of pure terror through me. That woman, with her veiled threats, knowing glances, and witch magic, was the last person I wanted Emily near.

"No," I said, my voice sharp, the fear and desperation I felt finally breaking through my carefully constructed façade. "You can't go to her."

Her chin lifted, her eyes blazing with a defiance that simultaneously thrilled and terrified me. "Then show me the note," she demanded, her voice unwavering.

Defeated, I gave her the crumpled note from my paw and placed it in her outstretched hand. My heart hammered against my ribs, a frantic drumbeat against the suffocating silence.

Her eyes scanned the brief message. The color leached from her face, leaving her skin pale and translucent in the fading light. A subtle tremor ran through her body, and her hand flew to her throat as if to ward off a sudden chill.

"Hand her over," she whispered, her voice barely audible, her eyes wide with dawning horror. "It's for her own good." She looked at me, her eyes filled with a desperate plea. "You won't... you won't do this, will you?"

"Never," I said, my voice thick with emotion, reaching out to steady her as she swayed. My arms instinctively wrapped around her, pulling her close, her warmth a welcome anchor in the storm raging within me. Holding her like this, feeling the frantic beat of her heart against my chest, ignited a fierce, primal protectiveness. I would burn the world down before I let anyone harm her.

"This..." she began, her voice trembling, "... this is about the wolf hunters, isn't it? And... and the others?"

I buried my face in her hair, inhaling the familiar scent of lavender and something uniquely her, a scent that both calmed and fueled my resolve. "Maybe… it's complicated," I admitted, my voice low and strained. The words were a bitter admission, a painful truth I had tried to shield her from.

A wave of guilt washed over me, heavy and suffocating. I had brought this danger into her life, exposing her to a world she was never meant to know. The thought of sending her back to her own time, away from me and the dangers of this world, was a physical pain, a tearing sensation in my chest. But it was perhaps the only way to keep her safe. Holding her close, I felt a surge of longing so intense it was almost unbearable, a desperate desire to protect her.

Even in the warmth of her embrace, I knew the path ahead was treacherous and uncertain, and the shadows were closing in.

"Come, we need to keep moving." I linked my arm with hers, nudged her forward, and sighed with relief when she followed, offering no resistance.

"Who?" she whispered.

"I don't know. It might not be related to time travel. I have enemies. But don't worry, I will keep you safe."

She tensed hearing my words. I should've been more tactful.

"Pretend to smile," I whispered. "Keep up the pretense that everything is all right." That was something I was well-versed in.

We continued walking, the silence punctuated by the clip-clop of horses' hooves on the paved path and the distant strains of a street musician's violin. The scent of roses, heavy and sweet, hung in the air, a stark contrast to the bitter taste of fear rising in my throat.

Passing a group huddled around a street performer, their laughter echoed unnaturally loud in the sudden stillness that had settled over us both.

A figure detached itself from the group, a dark shape against the fading light. He moved with a predatory grace, his gaze fixed on me. He nodded curtly, a barely perceptible movement, before melting back into the crowd.

A cold dread washed over me.

We were being watched.

CHAPTER 11

E mily

Nathaniel's paw, warm and firm against the small of my back, steered me through the throng of departing park-goers. A shiver, not entirely from the crisp autumn air, danced across my skin. The simple touch ignited a wildfire of sensation, painting my thoughts with forbidden possibilities.

When we made it to the park's edge, he gave curt instructions to the carriage driver, then assisted me into the carriage. My voluminous skirts, layers of silk and crinoline, proved a formidable obstacle. I stumbled slightly, catching myself on his arm, our fingers brushing. Heat flooded my cheeks.

Jeans would be better, I thought wistfully, tugging at the confining fabric. The corset, a rigid cage around my ribs, constricted my breath, mirroring the sudden tightness in my chest.

Once inside, I smoothed my skirts, acutely aware of Nathaniel settling onto the seat opposite. The enclosed space and his nearness amplified the awareness crackling between us. My pulse quickened. We were alone and hidden from the world.

The carriage lurched forward, the rhythmic clatter of hooves on cobblestones a stark contrast to the frantic drumming of my heart. A residue of fear, cold and clammy, still clung to me, but Nathaniel's presence was a steadying anchor in the storm. He gazed out the window, his jaw clenched, the familiar warmth of his smile replaced by a grim line.

"I haven't the faintest notion who would be behind this, Emily," he confessed, his voice tight with strain.

A wave of helplessness washed over me. "Maybe I should return home, Nathaniel," I suggested, touching the pendant. "If I could get it to work."

"Absolutely not," he retorted, his voice sharp with urgency. He turned to me, his gaze softening. "And you still have your father's work to finish, to stop the werewolf hunters." He paused, his expression darkening. "Besides, what if someone from your time knows about the pendant, Emily? What if they bring it back? Neither time is safe. We must assume that."

"That could be true." And I couldn't explain it, but I didn't want to go yet. There was so much to explore. This could be my only chance to discover more about what my father had been researching.

Reaching out, I covered his paw with my hand, needing to offer him comfort as much as I craved it myself. His fur was warm and soft beneath my fingertips. A jolt, unexpected and thrilling, shot through me at the contact. A yearning, unfamiliar and intense, bloomed within me.

I wanted more. Much more. I began to gently massage his paw, trying to ignore the strange, intoxicating desire that pulsed through my veins.

"There must be someone you can trust, Nathaniel," I said, my voice a little breathless, the words echoing the unspoken desires swirling within me. I tightened my grip on his paw, the warmth of his fur a comforting counterpoint to the icy fear that still lingered.

He stared out the window, his brow furrowed in thought. The silence stretched, punctuated only by the carriage wheels' rhythmic clatter and the muffled sounds of the city beyond.

"The theatre!" Turning to me, his voice was infused with a sudden, infectious excitement. "Don

Giovanni is playing at Her Majesty's Theatre tonight. There's a Goblin… Raziel… I could invite. He's high-born, discreet, and owes me a considerable favor." He spoke quickly, his words tumbling over each other in his eagerness. "I'll send him a coded message during the performance."

A thrill, sharp and exhilarating, coursed through me. "I knew you would think of something," I said, squeezing his paw gently, my heart swelling with admiration and affection.

He turned to me, his eyes alight with a warmth that sent a blush creeping up my neck. For a stolen moment, the fear and tension that had stretched taut between us dissolved. He leaned closer, his gaze intense, and I felt my breath catch in my throat, anticipation thrumming through me.

Then, with a jarring jolt, the carriage stopped, throwing me backward and forcing me to let go of his paw to brace myself from slipping from the seat. The fragile spell was broken.

Alistair opened the carriage door, his expression impassive. "Master Nathaniel, Miss Emily, welcome back."

Nathaniel stepped out, then turned and offered me his hand, his touch sending another unexpected shudder through me. I knew he wouldn't hand me over to whoever sent that note.

Nora waited for us at the entrance, her face a picture of concerned efficiency. "Nora…" Nathaniel instructed, his voice regaining its usual composure, "… please see that Miss Emily is prepared for the theatre this evening. I need to write a note."

"Of course, sir," Nora replied, her gaze flicking between us with a knowing look.

I wanted to go with him, to be at his side and offer him my support, just as he had offered me his. But Nora laid a gentle but firm hand on my arm. "Come along, Miss Emily," she said, steering me toward the grand staircase. "We'll need every minute to get you ready."

"Every minute?" I echoed incredulously. The thought of being separated from him, even for a few hours, filled me with a sudden unease.

Nora smiled, a hint of amusement in her eyes. "Indeed, Miss. A lady's toilette for the opera is not a matter to be rushed."

My heart ached to be with Nathaniel, to offer him my support, just as he had offered me his. But as Nora led me away, a chilling thought snaked its way into my mind, twisting the anticipation into a knot of fear. What if Nathaniel's message didn't reach Raziel in time? What if the danger lurking in the shadows was closer than we thought?

CHAPTER 12

*L*ord Nathaniel Blackwood

"Nora!" I called out, my voice echoing through the hallway. "Is Miss Emily ready? I don't wish to be late for Her Majesty's Theatre." *Don Giovanni* awaited, and more importantly, hopefully, my meeting with Raziel.

A moment later, Emily emerged from the top of the grand staircase. My inner wolf wanted to howl out in pleasure at what I saw.

The gown, a shimmering cascade of golden silk, flowed around her like liquid moonlight, accentuating the elegant curve of her neck and the delicate slope of her shoulders. Diamonds, glittering like captured stars, adorned her hair and the pendant safe around her neck. But it was her face, flushed with excitement and framed by the soft glow of the gaslight, that truly captivated me. She looked breathtaking.

"Emily…" I breathed out, "… you look absolutely stunning. Heads will turn tonight."

A mischievous glint sparked in her eyes. "Good," she purred, her voice laced with a newfound confidence that sent a wave of warmth through me. She was embracing this world, this life, with a spirit that both thrilled and terrified me. It was as if she was meant for this time and not the one she was born into.

I offered her my arm as she reached the bottom of the stairs, my heart pounding against my ribs. "Shall we?"

She linked her arm in mine with a grin that flared my desires, then I guided her outside where my private carriage awaited, its polished mahogany gleaming in the gaslight. Upholstered in burgundy velvet, the plush interior offered a welcome respite from the bustling city streets. As we settled into the soft cushions, I couldn't resist stealing another glance at her. The way the light played across her features and the subtle curve of her smile was intoxicating.

The ride to Her Majesty's Theatre was a blur of anticipation and stolen glances. I didn't trust myself to speak, let alone reach for her, as I thought I would explode in unbridled desire.

When we arrived, the sheer scale of the crowd gathered outside took Emily by surprise, and her eyes widened. Humans and non-humans alike, dressed in their finery, flooded the entrance, their voices a vibrant hum of excitement.

"You've never experienced anything like this in your time?" I asked, surprised. The theatre, opera, and social scene was all so integral to our world.

She shook her head, her gaze sweeping across the crowd. "Nothing quite like this."

I took her hand, helping her out of the carriage, then we made our way up the stairs to the theatre's entrance, enjoying the curious stares that followed us as we made our way through the throng. I had longed for a woman by my side, a companion to share these moments with. And now, here she was, radiant and captivating. The thought that it might be fleeting, that she might return to her own time, was a pang of regret I quickly pushed aside. Tonight, at least, she was mine.

Inside, I nodded greetings to acquaintances, savoring the envious glances cast our way. We reached my private booth, a secluded haven over-looking the stage.

The lights dimmed, and the orchestra began to play the opening chords of *Don Giovanni*. I settled back against the plush velvet, Emily beside me, her hand resting lightly on my paw.

The curtain rose, and the world outside faded away, replaced by the drama unfolding before us. Don Giovanni, the charismatic libertine, embarked on his path of seduction and deceit, his actions a stark reflection of the moral ambiguities that plagued our own lives. The music swelled, filling the private box, weaving a tapestry of desire and betrayal, mirroring the complex emotions that swirled between Emily and me.

I glanced at her, her face illuminated by the stage lights, her expression a mixture of fascination and unease. The opera, with its themes of forbidden love and hidden dangers, seemed to echo the precarious-ness of own situation, a reminder of the forces that both drew us together and threatened to tear us apart.

The final chords of the first act reverberated through the opera house, swallowed by a thunderous wave of applause. Though I'd diligently followed the performance, my attention kept returning to Emily at my side.

The house lights bloomed, signaling the intermission, and a subtle tension in my chest prompted me to rise. I scanned the crowds, not noticing any obvious threats. I hoped Raziel had received my note. But first, we needed to make an appearance, to keep up the social charade of being at the theatre.

"Champagne?" I murmured, the word barely audible above the din. My eyes met hers, and for a fleeting moment, the world narrowed to the space between us. The image of her lips, parted slightly, brushing the rim of a crystal flute, sent a wave of heat through me.

"Yes, thank you," she replied, her voice soft but clear. A smile touched her lips, and I felt my breath catch in my throat.

I extended my paw. Her fingers, cool and delicate, slipped into mine, sending a jolt of electricity up my arm. I guided her from the shadowed intimacy of our private box, the sudden brightness of the intermission lights momentarily blinding.

The grand foyer buzzed with a sea of elegantly dressed patrons, a kaleidoscope of silks and jewels. I felt a surge of protectiveness, the press of the crowd too close, too intimate.

"I can wait here if you like," Emily offered, her smile reassuring. "I'll be perfectly fine."

"Alone?" The word escaped me before I could

stop it, a hint of possessiveness I couldn't quite mask.

Her laughter, light and melodic, eased the tightness in my chest. "No one will hurt me here, Nathaniel. Surely you wouldn't bring me somewhere unsafe." Her eyes sparkled with amusement, and I felt a blush warm my cheeks.

"Of course not," I conceded, though the thought of leaving her unguarded, even for a moment, still pricked at me.

"Besides," she continued, her voice dropping to a conspiratorial whisper, "I can indulge in a little crowd-watching. It's simply fascinating. Look at what that woman is wearing!" Her gaze drifted across the foyer, a playful glint in her eyes. "Any lower, and her breasts will pop out."

A chuckle rumbled in my chest. I could picture Emily in a similarly daring gown, the thought sending a wave of heat through me. I needed to get away, to regain my composure before my desire betrayed me.

"I'll be quick," I promised, my voice a little rougher than intended. I turned toward the refreshment salon, the image of Emily surrounded by the glittering throng, a constant pull at the edge of my awareness.

The clinking of glasses and the low murmur of

conversation filled the refreshment salon. Two champagne flutes in hand, I nodded curtly to a few acquaintances, my thoughts already with Emily. I pushed through the throng, the delicate bubbles of the champagne a contrast to the anticipation simmering in my veins. Rounding the corner, my gaze sought out Emily where I had left her waiting.

My blood ran cold.

A figure, impeccably dressed yet radiating a predatory air, stood close to Emily, far too close. He leaned in, his attention riveted on something at her chest.

A primal surge of possessiveness roared through me, tightening my chest and sending the blood rushing to my ears. I practically lunged forward, the champagne flutes suddenly precarious in my grip.

As I drew nearer, I saw Emily lift her hand to her neck, adjusting the pendant nestled there. The seemingly innocent movement shifted the delicate chain, the pendant rising to momentarily reveal the soft curve of her breast beneath the gold silk of her gown. The man's hot and lingering gaze left no room for doubt—he'd been admiring far more than a family heirloom.

I reached them, the champagne flutes clicking together, the sound sharp in the sudden hush. I set them on a nearby table a little too forcefully, the delicate crystal ringing in protest. My eyes, cold and hard, locked onto the stranger's.

"My apologies for the delay," I clipped, my voice devoid of warmth.

He straightened, a flicker of surprise in his eyes before a smooth, practiced smile slid into place. "Indeed. I was merely admiring your… companion's exquisite pendant. A family heirloom, I understand."

Sensing the sudden freeze in the atmosphere, Emily looked from me to the stranger, apprehension clouding her eyes. "Lord Ashworth was just introducing himself," she explained, her voice a touch uncertain.

"Lord Ashworth," I echoed, the name tasting like acid on my tongue.

I moved deliberately, placing myself squarely between Emily and Ashworth, a silent but potent barrier. "Perhaps you might find other… *diversions* elsewhere. I believe my companion and I prefer to enjoy the remainder of the intermission… *privately*." The unspoken threat, thick with possessiveness, hung in the air, underscored by the rising swell of music signaling the imminent start of the second act.

The man's eyebrows rose a fraction, a flicker of amusement in his eyes. "My apologies. I merely wished to admire it more closely. Such possessiveness, sir. A commendable trait, perhaps, but one must be mindful of appearances in such refined company." His words, laced with a subtle mockery, pricked at my pride.

Emily, sensing the escalating tension, placed a reassuring hand over mine. "It's quite all right, Nathaniel," she murmured, her voice a calming balm against the rising storm within me. Yet, beneath her composed exterior, I detected a flicker of unease.

I forced a smile, though my eyes remained cold. "Indeed. But let us not forget that unchecked curiosity can sometimes lead to… unfortunate consequences."

The man chuckled a low, predatory sound that grated on my nerves. "A veiled threat? How intriguing." He bowed again, his gaze lingering on Emily for a beat too long. "Very well. I shall leave you to your… *enjoyment*." He turned and melted back into the crowd, leaving a palpable tension in his wake.

As the lights dimmed once more, signaling the start of the second act, I leaned closer to Emily, my voice low and urgent. "Be wary, Emily. Not everyone here tonight has honorable intentions."

*E*mily

The house lights faded, leaving the stage a jewel box of light and shadow. I sank back into the plush velvet, the warmth doing little to thaw the chill that had settled over me since I'd spoken to Lord Ashworth. Had I been careless? He'd seemed so nice.

Beside me, Nathaniel sat perfectly still, a statue carved from moonlight and shadow. I could feel his presence like a physical weight, amplifying my unease.

My gaze drifted to the glittering diamond necklace of the woman seated in the adjacent box, then to the ruby pendant dangling precariously low on the chest of another. Just moments ago, I'd been so enthralled by this spectacle of wealth and fashion, so eager to absorb every detail, to prove I belonged in this rarefied world. Now, the same display felt suffocating, a gaudy reminder of my lapse in judgment.

Lord Ashworth's face, etched with an irresistible charm, flashed before my eyes. I could still feel the weight of his gaze, hot and lingering where it shouldn't have been at my cleavage. The ghost of it sent a shiver down my spine, the soft silk of my gown suddenly feeling thin and inadequate. I'd let my guard down.

I risked a sideways glance at Nathaniel. His jaw was tight, the line of his profile sharp against the dim light. He stared straight ahead, seemingly absorbed by the performance, but the rigid set of his shoulders betrayed him, along with the movement of his eyes, always scanning the audience.

I remembered the way he'd inserted himself between Ashworth and me, the controlled fury in his voice, the barely veiled threat. The memory sent a strange thrill through me, a flicker of heat in the cold dread. Yet, beneath the thrill, a disquiet remained. The air between us crackled with unspoken words, a tension stretched taut like a violin string. The easy camaraderie we'd shared earlier had vanished, replaced by something brittle.

The orchestra swelled, a cascade of notes washing over me, but the music felt distant and distorted. On stage, the soprano hit a high note, her voice ringing with passion, but the sound barely registered. My mind was a battlefield, Lord Ashworth's oily smile clashing with the memory of Nathaniel's steely gaze. Shame coiled in my stomach, a bitter taste rising in my throat. I'd been so eager to impress, so desperate to fit in, that I'd practically offered myself up on a silver platter. And now, the price of my ignorance hung heavily in the air between Nathaniel and me.

The silence between us stretched, thick with unspoken words. I stared at the stage, unseeing, my fingers twisting in my lap.

Then, a warmth brushed against my hand. I flinched, then looked down. Nathaniel's paw, large and strong, covered mine.

The unexpected contact sent a ripple of awareness through me, a jolt of something that felt startlingly like electricity. I held my breath, hyperaware of the texture of his fur against my skin and the warmth that radiated from him.

It was a simple gesture, yet it spoke volumes. An

apology, perhaps? Or a silent reassurance? Or maybe, just maybe, something more.

I focused on the feeling of his paw in mine, the steady beat of his pulse a counterpoint to the frantic rhythm of my heart. The heat of his touch spread slowly through me, chasing away the chill that had settled deep in my bones. The tight knot of anxiety in my stomach began to loosen, replaced by a strange, fluttering warmth. I inhaled deeply, the scent of velvet and the faintest hint of Nathaniel's spicy cologne filling my lungs.

The music, which had been a distant blur, began to sharpen, the soaring melodies weaving their way back into my consciousness. The soprano's voice, filled with longing and despair, resonated with a depth I hadn't noticed before. On stage, the lovers embraced, their bodies entwined in a passionate dance. I found myself drawn into their story, the earlier turmoil receding like the tide pulling back from the shore.

Nathaniel's paw, a solid anchor in the swirling sea of my emotions, grounded me in the present. I found myself leaning into him, almost imperceptibly at first, drawn to the solid strength of his shoulder. In the quiet intimacy of our shared space, nestled beside Nathaniel, I felt safe.

The final, dramatic chords reverberated through

the hall, the curtain falling on the lovers' final embrace. A wave of applause erupted, washing over us, a tangible expression of the audience's shared experience.

As the actors took their bows, beaming and breathless, a small, folded note appeared, seemingly out of nowhere, delivered by a liveried usher directly to Nathaniel. He unfolded it with a frown, his brow furrowing as he scanned the brief message. The sudden shift in his demeanor, the tightening of his jaw, sent a ripple of unease through me.

He refolded the note, his movements precise and economical, and turned to me, his expression unreadable. "We need to leave," he said, his voice low and urgent, cutting through the celebratory chatter around us.

A flicker of apprehension danced in my chest. "Now?" I asked, my voice barely above a whisper, the sudden change of plans jarring me from the tranquil space I'd just found. "Is everything all right?"

His paw tightened around my hand, a brief, reassuring squeeze. "It's time to meet him," he murmured, his gaze sweeping over the crowd, a subtle tension in his stance.

"The goblin?" I asked, and he nodded. The excitement and magic of the evening evaporated, giving way to a growing sense of urgency.

Nathaniel guided me through the throng of departing patrons, the glittering foyer suddenly feeling less enchanting and more ominous. I followed him, my hand clasped tightly in his, hoping that whatever awaited us outside the gilded doors of the opera house wouldn't shatter the fragile peace we'd found in the darkness within.

CHAPTER 14

$\mathcal{L}$ord Nathaniel Blackwood

The final applause washed over me, a hollow echo against the growing unease in my chest. Emily's hand remained nestled in mine, a comforting warmth I was loath to relinquish. But the discreetly delivered note, tucked into my palm by the usher, had shattered the fragile peace of the moment. It was time to meet Raziel, and I didn't like how late he'd left it to respond to me.

My focus shifted, the glittering spectacle of the opera house fading into the background as a new, more urgent concern took hold. I needed to know what awaited us beyond these walls, and I wouldn't leave Emily vulnerable again, not even in a place I'd previously considered safe.

"Stay close," I murmured to Emily, my voice low, drawing her closer as I scanned the opulent foyer.

Her eyes, wide and questioning, met mine. A flicker of concern crossed her features, but she nodded, her trust a silent affirmation. I tightened my grip on her hand, unwilling to let go, even for a moment.

I guided her through the thinning crowd, my senses heightened, alert for any sign of Raziel. The air buzzed with post-performance chatter, the scent of perfume and expensive cigars hanging heavily in the air. Near the grand staircase, beneath the watchful gaze of a marble cherub, I spotted him.

Raziel, the goblin, blended seamlessly into the crowd, his impeccable evening attire a stark contrast to the shady dealings of his life beneath his polished veneer. He raised a gloved hand in a subtle greeting, his eyes, ancient and knowing, holding my gaze.

I approached him, Emily at my side, my steps measured and purposeful. "Raziel," I greeted casually, my voice a low murmur, barely audible above the surrounding din.

"Nathaniel," he replied, a hint of amusement playing on his lips. He inclined his head toward Emily. "And…"

"Emily," I supplied, drawing her closer to my side. "She stays with me."

Raziel's eyebrow arched slightly, but he offered a polite nod. "Pleased to meet you."

"Can you tell me who is controlling the shadows?" I responded, my tone clipped.

His smile faded, replaced by a look of grave concern. "Concerning developments, I'm afraid. A new faction is emerging, humans dabbling in powers they don't understand, hungry for power and time travel."

My jaw tightened. "Humans?" I questioned, a surge of unease tightening my gut. "Details, Raziel. I need specifics."

Raziel sighed, a sound like rustling leaves. "They're high-born and have money, that's for sure, but they want more. They want to change outcomes and are looking to time travel to do this. It's been difficult to get this from them."

"Who are they?" I asked impatiently.

"Their identities are elusive. I've yet to uncover any key figures."

Frustration gnawed at me. "We can't afford to wait. This unchecked ambition could destabilize everything. If they start messing around with time travel, they could well end up ruling over London with iron fists."

"Or ruling the world," Emily added.

"Indeed," Raziel agreed, his gaze darkening. "The balance is precarious. This new element throws everything into chaos." He paused, his eyes searching mine. "Be cautious, Nathaniel. They are dangerous and hunger for power like I've never encountered before."

I nodded, the weight of his words settling heavily on my shoulders. "I'll be vigilant. Keep me informed."

"And keep her safe." With a final, almost imperceptible nod, Raziel vanished back into the throng of opera-goers, swallowed by the opulent surroundings as if he were a phantom himself.

The news he'd brought settled like a leaden cloak on my shoulders, the threat of unknown enemies a cold, creeping dread. Yet, as my gaze fell upon Emily, a different kind of warmth spread through me, a fierce protectiveness that mingled with a growing admiration.

"We have to find out who these people are," she said softly, her voice barely audible above the receding tide of departing guests. She leaned closer, her shoulder brushing against mine, her nearness a tangible comfort.

A dangerous idea, a reckless gamble, sparked in

my mind. "Do you trust me?" I asked, my voice low and intense, my gaze searching hers.

Her answer was immediate, unwavering. "I do."

"Then listen closely," I said, my grip tightening on her hand. "We're going to walk the promenade. It might draw them out, if they're here tonight." My voice dropped to a near whisper. "I hate to put you in danger, but…"

"Let's go," she interrupted, her voice firm, laced with quiet determination that surprised and thrilled me.

"Really?" I asked, a flicker of disbelief, and a surge of something akin to pride, coursing through me.

"Yes," she replied, a hint of impatience in her tone. "Come on, what's taking you so long?" A faint smile played on her lips, a spark of defiance in her eyes.

I stared at her for a heartbeat, captivated by her courage and unwavering confidence. This woman was incredible.

A wave of something intense, something beyond admiration, washed over me. I wanted to protect her, yes, but I also wanted her. The realization struck me with the force of a physical blow, leaving me breathless.

Taking a deep breath, I steered her toward the

grand exit, toward the Moonlight Promenade. The weight of Raziel's warning still pressed heavily on my mind, and here I was doing the exact opposite.

$\mathcal{E}$mily

The opera house doors released us into the cool night air, a stark contrast to the gilded warmth we'd just left. The lingering excitement of the performance now vibrated with a different energy, a thrum of anticipation tinged with danger that emanated from Nathaniel. His paw gripped my hand tightly, a reassuring warmth, yet his gaze darted around, constantly scanning the crowd. I could feel the tension radiating from him, a silent current that flowed between us.

We turned onto the promenade, bathed in the moon's soft glow. A warning whispered in the back of my mind—*beware the Moonlight Promenade*—the words clear in my father's journal. But I didn't tell Nathaniel. I couldn't. He needed to do this, and I needed him to. We had to uncover who was manipulating the shadows and pulling the strings of this need to change events in time in order to gain power.

The air filled with the murmur of voices, the rustle of silks and satins, the gentle clip-clop of horses' hooves on the cobblestones. Couples strolled arm in arm, their laughter echoing in the night. Groups of friends chatted animatedly, their faces flushed with wine and the thrill of the performance. Could any of these seemingly ordinary people be one of *them?*

In the midst of it all, Nathaniel's awareness, his paw in my hand, and his body so close I could feel the heat radiating from him added another layer of complexity to the already charged atmosphere. It was intoxicating.

As we rounded a bend in the path on the Moonlight Promenade bathed in the ethereal glow of the just full moon, I caught a flash of movement in the manicured flowerbeds that bordered the path.

It wasn't human.

Three figures, slender and graceful, with skin that shimmered like moonlight on water, flitted among the roses. Their light and musical laughter reached my ears, a stark contrast to the human sounds around us. Fae. I breathed out, almost giggling as I realized they didn't pose a threat.

They paused, their luminous eyes meeting mine for a fleeting moment, before they vanished into the shadows as quickly and silently as they had appeared. Their energy, infectious and buoyant, helped to release the tension.

A moment later, two figures emerged from the ancient oak tree that stood sentinel at the edge of the promenade. Their skin was the color of bark, their hair a tangle of leaves and vines. Dryads, guardians of the trees, the knowledge came to me easily from years of research into folklore.

They exchanged a knowing glance with Nathaniel, a silent acknowledgment, before melting back into the oak trunk, becoming one with the wood. This world, I realized, was far more complex than I had ever imagined, a tapestry woven with threads of magic and mystery, with hidden creatures lurking just beneath the surface of the mundane. And Nathaniel, with his secrets and his powers, was clearly a part of it. Did I want to be part of it? To be part of what I had read instead of thinking it was a fantasy?

The thought sent a shiver down my spine, a cold

finger tracing its way along my nerves. I glanced at Nathaniel, his profile sharp and determined in the moonlight.

He seemed so sure, so in control. His confidence, his unwavering belief in our purpose, helped to push my fear aside.

For some reason, that felt right. More than right. It felt exciting.

Dangerous, yes, but also exhilarating. Being near him, sharing this purpose, ignited a spark within me, a warmth that spread through my chest, chasing away the chill of the night. This was more than just a night at the opera, it was a plunge into the heart of a mystery. And for the first time, I felt truly alive.

A sudden shift in his demeanor, a subtle tightening of his grip on my hand, pulled me from my thoughts. He'd stopped walking, his body tensed, his gaze fixed on something beyond my peripheral vision.

I followed his line of sight but saw nothing out of the ordinary. Just the Moonlight Promenade, the strolling couples, the gentle murmur of conversation. Then, I felt it—a subtle shift in the air, a prickling sensation on the back of my neck. Someone or something was watching us.

A soft snarl vibrated deep within Nathaniel's throat as he stalked closer, his approach a graceful menace, and I followed him, keeping close. "You shouldn't be so trusting," he cautioned, his voice a seductive rumble, a velvet-wrapped threat. His golden eyes flickered with a tumult of emotions, belying his stern warning.

"But I am," I confessed, my voice barely a breath, resolve crumbling under the intensity of his gaze. An inexplicable force pulled me toward him, bridging the distance despite the primal fear that danced in my veins. "I feel safe with you."

Nathaniel's composure momentarily fractured. His clawed paw hovered, a hair's breadth from my face, before gently tracing the curve of my cheek. The touch of his paw, fur soft against my skin, sent a shiver down my spine, a delightful torment that defined every stolen moment with him.

"You turn me inside out, Emily," he murmured, raw honesty lacing his tone. "How can you trust a creature like me?"

"Because I see the kindness in you, Nathaniel. Not the beast others perceive, but the gentle soul within." I covered his paw with my hand, pressing it closer, burying my fingers in the soft fur.

A low growl rumbled in his chest, this time laced with vulnerability. He pulled me into his embrace, powerful arms a haven against the strangeness of this time and place. His lips found mine, desperate and hungry. His canines grazed my upper lip, a tantalizing promise of the passion to come, and I shivered, yearning for more.

His kiss was a wildfire, tender yet consuming, and I clung to him, wanting to explore the hard planes of his chest beneath the fabric of his vest, the power in the muscles that bunched beneath my fingertips. When he finally broke the kiss, a ragged sigh escaped him, his warm breath ghosting across my lips. He pressed his forehead against mine, our bodies still flush against each other.

"Be careful, Emily," he warned, his voice thick with unspoken emotion. "This… between us… it could destroy us both."

His words were a warning, but in his embrace, a reckless hope bloomed within me, fierce and untamed. "Then let it," I whispered, my voice trembling with newfound courage.

Then I felt it, not the bliss I had been expecting, but the draining pull I had felt before.

"They're here." I pulled away from Nathaniel.

The other people on the promenade seemed oblivious, their laughter and conversation continuing as if nothing were amiss. But I could see these creatures of darkness, their eyes burning with an unholy light, pinpoints of malevolence in the swirling gloom. The shadows were coming for me.

Nathaniel snarled, a low, guttural sound that vibrated through me. He pushed me back, his paw firm against my lower back. "Run, Emily! *Now!*"

Terror, cold and sharp, pierced through the haze of desire. This wasn't a game, a flirtation with danger. This was real. Heart-poundingly, terrifyingly real. And I was in the middle of it, caught between the encroaching shadows and the man who had both drawn me in and now pushed me away for my safety.

We had to get out of there. My lungs screamed, the elegant skirts tangling around my legs, heels sinking into the uneven cobblestones. Each stride was a clumsy fight. He grabbed my hand, his grip surprisingly gentle despite the urgency.

"Down here!" he barked, pulling me into a narrow alley. The stench of stale refuse and something else, something sickly sweet and *wrong*, filled the air. "Keep running!"

The shadows were close, too close. I felt a sickening drain, my energy leaching away as they fed.

"Keep going." He let go of my hand and stopped, turning to face the enemy.

I ran, desperate to obey even though every instinct screamed for me to stay with him.

"Get away!" he roared from behind me.

My breath burned in my lungs, my feet pounding

the cobblestones as I fled down the dark alley. I risked a glance over my shoulder.

The shadows weren't just swarming him, they were *on* him, tearing at his cloak, shadowy claws raking across his back. He roared, a sound both human and animal as golden light pulsed beneath the fabric.

It wasn't the clean explosion I'd expected.

It flickered, sputtered, and threatened to be extinguished by the sheer number of attackers.

The creatures shrieked, their forms dissolving into smoke, but more kept coming, an endless tide of darkness. He staggered, one hand clutching his side, crimson staining his fingers. I wanted to run back to help him, but terror rooted me to the spot.

Then, a new, deeper growl ripped through the night, and the golden light flared again, this time stronger, fiercer, pushing the shadows back. But even as they retreated, I saw it, a flicker of something dark and hungry in his eyes.

He'd done it. Relief surged through me, and I started to run back, but something caught my eye.

Standing at the edge of the promenade, where the alley began, was a figure I recognized with a sickening twist in my stomach—Lord Ashworth. He watched with a chillingly detached amusement.

He had to be the one controlling the shadows. We weren't safe.

"Keep going!" Nathaniel urged as he rushed to my side, gripping my hand firmly. He guided me into the maze of alleys, pushing us deeper into the darkness, closer to the sanctuary of his home.

$\mathcal{E}$mily

The front door slammed shut, the *thud* vibrating through the floor and up into my chest, starkly contrasting the sudden silence of his home. It was as if a dam had burst, not just broken, releasing the pent-up terror and adrenaline. My lungs seized, each breath a ragged, painful effort. *Breathe. Just breathe.* But the air wouldn't come. Then, I turned to him.

The world narrowed, shrinking to Nathaniel's solid, reassuring presence. He was an anchor in the swirling chaos of my fear. Before thought could form, before reason could intervene, I was in his arms. His lips crashed down on mine, hard, demanding, a collision of desperate need.

I couldn't get close enough. Clumsy with urgency, my hands fumbled with his shirt buttons, finally ripping it free from his trousers. I had to feel him, the solid warmth of his back, the taut muscles flexing beneath the surprisingly soft fur. It was a grounding touch, a lifeline in the swirling chaos, but it wasn't enough. Not nearly enough.

A gasp tore from my lips, a sound of pure, unfiltered pleasure. The feel of his skin, the raw power beneath my fingertips, was intoxicating, overwhelming. The lingering fear was a distant hum, drowned out by the roar of desire that consumed me.

He was safety.

He was danger.

He was *everything*.

His paws, possessive and strong, circled my waist, then traced a burning path up my spine, each touch a spark igniting a wildfire within me. They dipped lower, cupping my backside through the layers of my skirts, his touch a jolt of pure, electric need. He squeezed, a possessive, almost painful pressure that stretched and pulled, sending a wave of exquisite sensation through my intimate folds. A whimper escaped me, a plea and a surrender all in one.

A low, guttural growl vibrated in his chest, a sound of primal frustration. He pulled back slightly, his dark and molten eyes locked on mine. "Not here," he rasped, the words barely a whisper.

I didn't have time to process or question. He swept me into his arms, the sudden movement stealing my breath. I was weightless, adrift, the lingering terror of the alley replaced by the dizzying anticipation of what was to come.

He carried me through the darkness, a journey of blurred shadows and the intoxicating scent of musk and something wilder, something untamed. Then, with a reverence that belied the raw hunger in his eyes, he lowered me onto the yielding softness of his bed.

A dizzying wave of anticipation, fueled by the lingering electricity of his touch, crashed over me. His lips devoured mine, demanding, possessive, and I met his hunger with a ferocity that surprised even me. I was lost, adrift in the sea of him—the musky scent of his skin, the soft rasp of fur against my fingertips, the raw, undeniable *power* emanating from him.

He pushed up my skirts, a rough, impatient gesture, his paws tracing a burning path along the sensitive skin of my thighs. A gasp escaped me, a sound of pure, unfiltered pleasure. Then, his tongue flickered out, a hot, wet caress against the slick folds between my legs, and I groaned, my hips bucking involuntarily. *More*. I needed *more*.

His mouth pressed against my core, his tongue a relentless, a driving force that sent shock waves of sensation through my entire body. I reached behind me, fingers clutching the pillows, anchoring myself against the rising tide of pleasure. My hips arched, offering myself to him, and he rewarded me with a deep, probing lick that sent a jolt of pure ecstasy straight to my core.

His tongue danced, a wicked, knowing rhythm that drew every drop of moisture from me, before settling on the swollen bud of my clit, circling, teasing, tormenting until I convulsed, a cry torn from my throat as wave after wave of release crashed over me.

He moved away, leaving me breathless and trembling. I sat up, my hands sliding around his neck, drawing him close until our noses almost touched, our breaths mingling, hot and ragged. "Get. Your. Clothes. Off," he growled, the words a low vibration against my ear, a command and a promise.

I didn't need to be told twice. I shimmied off the bed, a molten heat pooling between my thighs, and turned my attention to the cursed corset, my arms twisting awkwardly behind me. He shed his shirt and trousers with an impatient grace while I struggled with the intricate ties, turning my back to him.

"How am I *meant* to do this?" Frustration, sharp and stinging, cut through the haze of desire. I wanted him, *needed* him, skin to fur, the raw, animal heat of him against me, *now*. This damned contraption was a barrier, a torture.

"Stand still." He turned me, and I melted against him, the plush, heated fur of his chest a welcome shock against my bare back. His paws encircled me, possessive and strong, the soft pads tracing the curve of my belly, igniting a wildfire within. His touch climbed higher, cupping my breasts, flicking across my already-hardened nipples, sending jolts of pure pleasure straight to my core. I arched back, pressing myself against him, the hard, insistent length of his erection a tantalizing pressure against the cleft of my buttocks, teasing, promising. A moan escaped me, low and throaty.

I was a raw, throbbing ache, desperate for the release only he could provide, but he seemed intent on prolonging the exquisite torment, a master of anticipation. One paw remained possessively cupping my breast, kneading and teasing the already-hardened nipple, while the other slid lower, delving into the slick, molten heat between my legs.

A gasp tore from my throat as his paw found the swollen bud of my clit, circling, stroking with a practiced skill that bordered on supernatural. My fingers dug into the thick fur of his shoulders, anchoring myself against the rising tide of sensation. His hot breath, a ragged, panting rhythm, ghosted across my shoulder, a whispered promise of the pleasure to come.

Then, a sharp, exquisite sting on my shoulder pierced the haze, a jolt that sharpened my senses. His teeth grazed my flesh, a possessive bite, both thrilling and terrifying, a mark that branded me as his. In that instant, any lingering doubt, any shred of hesitation, evaporated. I was his, completely—body and soul. I trusted him, *craved* him, with a primal intensity that defied logic.

He lifted me effortlessly, settling me back onto the bed, the plush fur beneath me a welcome contrast to the fevered heat of my skin. I reached for him, a desperate, clinging embrace, my legs instinctively wrapping around his waist, locking him close. His erection, thick and hard, pressed against me, slick with my arousal, a tantalizing prelude. Then, with a guttural groan that was both pleasure and surrender, he thrust forward, sinking into me. I arched upward, my body a welcoming vessel, my muscles parting instinctively, then clenching around him, a tight, milking grip that savored the exquisite fullness, the *rightness* of him inside me.

He pulled back, almost completely withdrawing, drawing a desperate whimper from my lips as a bolt of raw sensation ripped through me. Then, before I could even gasp for air, he plunged back in, burying himself to the hilt, the feeling both exquisitely agonizing and overwhelmingly perfect.

We moved as one, a primal, untamed rhythm, a dance of desperate need. Each thrust was a lightning strike, each touch a brand, a reaffirmation of the bond that had forged between us, hotter and stronger than any flame. The world outside, with its dangers and uncertainties, dissolved. There was only *him*, the rough, plush feel of his fur against my slick skin, the scorching heat of his body engulfing mine, and the overwhelming, all-consuming need to be closer, to be *consumed*, to be utterly lost in him.

We lay tangled in the sweat-soaked sheets, the aftershocks of pleasure still rippling through me, a warm, languid embrace. His paw traced the curve of my skin, moving up over my shoulder, then he paused, his touch lingering on the throbbing, sensitive mark of his teeth.

"I'm sorry," he murmured, his voice a low rumble.

"Don't," I breathed out, the word a shaky exhale. But I felt it, a subtle shift in him, a flicker of something beyond desire. In that moment, cradled in his arms, the mark felt not like a wound, but a brand, a symbol of belonging, a declaration of *possession* that I welcomed and craved.

*L*ord Nathaniel Blackwood

I didn't want her to leave. Not my bed, not my arms, not ever. Her body, still flushed and warm from our lovemaking, lay nestled against mine, a perfect fit. I couldn't resist running a paw through her silken hair, savoring the soft, sleepy murmur of contentment she made. It was a sound I wanted to hear every morning for the rest of my existence.

"We *should* get up," I murmured, the words a lie even to my ears. A sliver of sunlight, defiant and bright, pierced the edge of the heavy curtains, a reminder of the world outside, a world I wanted to keep at bay. Here, in this bed, with her, was all that mattered.

"No… stay," she mumbled, her voice thick with sleep and lingering pleasure. She pressed closer, her body molding against mine, and the embers of desire, still smoldering from the night before, rekindled with a fierce intensity. My cock, already stirring, hardened fully against her thigh.

I reached for her, claiming her mouth in a deep, possessive kiss. Her tongue met mine, a playful, teasing dance, a delightful contrast to the sharp, almost painful nip of her teeth on my lower lip. The combination sent a jolt of pure lust through me, straight to my core.

With a sinuous, feline grace, she rolled on top of me, straddling my belly. I felt myself sink deep inside her, enveloped and held fast by the rhythmic clench of her inner muscles. Her breasts, round and heavy, swayed tantalizingly close, their nipples taut, dark peaks that seemed to beckon my touch. Almost of their own volition, my paws rose, drawn to their fullness, and as I cupped their weight against my soft pads, she arched back with a throaty groan, pressing herself more firmly against me.

A primal urge surged through me. I eased out my claws, just the very tips, pressing them *lightly* into the delicate skin of her breasts, a possessive, almost painful caress. She rewarded me with a gasp, a surge of wetness, and the exquisite clenching of her inner muscles around my still-embedded cock.

A sharp, insistent knock on the door shattered the moment, making her tense, her body stiffening above me. A growl rumbled in my chest, a primal urge to *roar*, to send whoever dared interrupt us fleeing in terror. Instead, Emily, bless her defiant spirit, ground her hips down, rocking against me with a slow, deliberate rhythm. I groaned, a sound of pure, desperate pleasure, and thrust upward, burying myself deeper inside her, seeking the hot, wet haven she so readily offered.

The knock came again, louder this time, more demanding.

"My Lord…" a muffled voice called, laced with a hesitant urgency.

"Come back later," I growled, my voice thick with residual lust and a possessive edge. I relinquished control, letting her dictate the rhythm, my hands moving to her hips, not to command, but to guide, to *enhance*. She understood, her movements became more deliberate, each downward plunge driving me deeper, her inner muscles milking me, a tight, exquisite grip that bordered on painful pleasure.

"It's… urgent, my Lord." The voice, strained and

insistent, penetrated the haze of our passion, but barely.

"It can wait… just… a… *moment*," I managed to gasp, the words fragmented by the sheer intensity of the sensation. I thrust upward, meeting her halfway, harder, faster, knowing, *feeling* her nearing the edge. A strangled cry escaped her lips, her body shuddering, convulsing around me as she reached her peak. Her release triggered my own, a volcanic eruption that sent wave after wave of pure, unadulterated pleasure coursing through me. I spilled myself deep inside her, a primal, possessive act.

We lay entwined, breathless, slick with sweat, the afterglow a warm, heavy blanket, a shared space of perfect contentment.

"Morning sex… is definitely… the best," she mumbled, her voice a drowsy purr, nuzzling her face against the fur of my chest, her breath warm against my skin.

"Undeniably," I agreed, my voice still rough with the remnants of passion. I couldn't resist stroking her hair, the silken strands a delightful contrast to the rough pads of my paws.

"Lord!" The door rattled again, the sound a jarring intrusion, a threat to our perfect bubble.

I groaned, a low rumble of frustration vibrating in my chest. "Coming!" I called out, the word laced with reluctance. I kissed her, a lingering, tender press of my lips to hers, then, with a supreme effort of will, helped her off me. The sight of her, naked and flushed, standing before me, almost made me reconsider answering the door at all.

"I protest this interruption," she declared, a playful pout on her lips, but a spark of genuine annoyance in her eyes.

"Rightly so, Emily," I agreed, my voice still husky. The sound of her name on my tongue sent a fresh wave of possessiveness through me. "But, unfortunately, we do have the rather pressing matter of those shadows that seem intent on ending your existence, and, well…" I added, a playful growl rumbling in my chest, "… I now have *exceptionally* compelling and deeply personal motives to ensure your continued survival."

I couldn't resist a final, playful swat to her gloriously bare backside before grabbing my trousers, the fine wool a poor substitute for the feel of her skin. The need to reclaim her and pull her back into bed was almost overwhelming.

"Fine." She sighed with a hint of playful resignation in her voice and a clear reluctance to break our intimate bubble. She moved toward the discarded pile of clothing, creating a much-needed, yet agonizing, distance between us. "Though I'm afraid 'getting dressed' is going to be a rather significant challenge." She picked up the shredded remains of the corset, a tangible reminder of my possessive frenzy from the night before.

"I'll send Nora up to assist you," I offered, my voice still thick with the remnants of desire.

"Thank you, but perhaps something… less constricting would be more practical," she suggested, tossing the ruined corset back onto the floor with a delicate shudder.

A wave of heat, a potent cocktail of lust and possessiveness, washed over me. The memory of tearing that garment from her body, the feel of the fabric ripping beneath my claws, the sight of her exposed skin—it was an intensely arousing image. Perhaps these archaic contraptions *did* have a purpose beyond mere societal constraint. They were instruments of delicious torment, for the wearer and, most definitely, for the one privileged enough to remove them.

As she turned, the faint, purplish-blue bruising on her shoulder, a constellation of my teeth marks, caught my eye. My gut clenched, a fist of guilt and anxiety twisting in my stomach.

She didn't understand. She couldn't possibly grasp the significance of what I'd done. I *shouldn't* have marked her. It was a reckless, impulsive act, driven by instinct, by the primal urge to claim her, to brand her as *mine*. She wasn't of this time, and this possessive act, so deeply ingrained in my nature, might have consequences I couldn't foresee. The last thing I wanted was to create a bond that would prevent her return to her own time, to her own life.

But it was too late.

The mark was there, *my* mark, a visible manifestation of our connection, a connection that now felt both exhilarating and terrifyingly fragile. The thought of separation, of the agonizing pain it would inflict on us, now that we were so inextricably linked, was a physical ache, a throbbing pressure in my chest. I should have been more controlled, more considerate, but the raw, overwhelming need to possess her and make her irrevocably mine, had overridden all reason.

I forced myself to focus, buttoning my shirt with trembling fingers. I needed to regain control to think clearly. I went to the door, the movement stiff and unnatural. Muffled whispers from the other side, hushed and urgent, pricked my curiosity.

Normally, I would have demanded to know what was happening, protocol be damned. But my half-dressed state and the turmoil raging within me made me hesitate. Besides, I was certain the entire household would soon be aware of Emily's presence and my involvement with her. It hardly mattered.

I was reaching for the door handle when it swung inward, revealing a servant, his face pale and drawn, holding a folded note. He thrust it toward me, his hand trembling slightly. The dark, almost fearful expression in his eyes mirrored the sudden dread that coiled in my gut as I unfolded the paper and scanned the hastily scrawled message.

"What is it?" Emily asked, her voice laced with a concern that cut through my rising panic.

"It's… nothing serious," I lied, the words like ash in my mouth. "Just a business deal that's threatening to go sour. I need to attend to it immediately before I lose a considerable portion of my fortune."

I shoved the note into my pocket, a desperate attempt to conceal the truth that I knew was reflected in my eyes. This wasn't about business or the shadows, but the escalating threat they posed, a threat that now felt terrifyingly real, terrifyingly *close*.

"I'll send Nora up with some fresh clothes," I mumbled, backing away, my voice strained, my movements abrupt. I needed to escape, to put distance between us, not just to cool the lingering heat in my blood, but to process the chilling implications of the note, and to formulate a plan to protect her.

"Of course, my Lord," the servant replied, his voice barely audible as he retreated down the hallway.

I needed space, air, a moment to breathe and think before the suffocating weight of my fear and my love for her completely consumed me.

I unfolded the crumpled paper, the stark, menacing words a chilling echo of the danger that coiled around us, tightening its grip. *We want her. Bring her to the docks at 2 a.m., or you will lose her forever, and your own life. Bring the pendant.*

Surrendering Emily was *unthinkable*. An act so vile, so contrary to every fiber of my being, that the mere suggestion ignited a cold fury within me. Relinquishing the pendant, an artifact of immense power and historical significance, was equally abhorrent. But the alternative—risking Emily's life—was a torment I couldn't bear. The thought twisted in my gut, a venomous serpent coiling around my heart.

I strode out of the manor, the gravel crunching beneath my boots, each step a physical manifestation of my racing, desperate thoughts. The late morning sunlight, harsh and unforgiving, assaulted my eyes, accustomed to the dim, intimate light of the bedroom.

The fresh, crisp breeze whipped around me, offering a momentary reprieve. I needed clarity, a plan, a *weapon*. The sprawling grounds of my estate, still shrouded in the lingering shadows of dawn, seemed to offer the only solace I could find.

As I walked around my gardens, a strategy, born of desperation and fueled by a fierce, protective rage, began to coalesce in my mind. These creatures, whoever they were, clearly possessed resources, knowledge, and a chilling disregard for human life.

But they underestimated *me*.

They underestimated the lengths I would go to protect what was *mine*. They wanted the pendant, and they wanted Emily. They would receive *neither*.

I would meet them, yes, but on *my* terms, under *my* control. A twisted smile played on my lips. Emily would remain here, safely ensconced within the manor's protective embrace, far from their grasping claws. And the pendant, the object of their avarice, the key they believed would unlock unimaginable power? It would be nothing but smoke and mirrors, a meticulously crafted illusion, a phantom designed to buy me precious time, time to dismantle their plans, to turn their arrogance and greed against them. They sought to use her as leverage. They would find only a carefully laid trap.

I snatched the crumpled note from my pocket, the coarse paper a tangible reminder of their audacity, their threat. I reread the stark, demanding words, letting the cold fury rise within me, fueling my resolve. Then, with a deliberate, almost theatrical gesture, I crushed the note in my fist and flung it into the wind, watching the scraps of paper dance and scatter like frightened birds. The message was irrelevant now.

I could engineer a device for distraction, one that, when activated, would emit a high-pitched, almost inaudible frequency, specifically calibrated to disorient, disrupt, or momentarily incapacitate. I could strategically plant these around the docks, creating a web of chaos and confusion, a sonic shield that would provide me with the crucial window I needed to neutralize the immediate threat and to turn the hunters into the hunted.

My heightened senses, the primal instincts of my wolf form, sharpened by the urgency of the situation, would be my greatest advantage. I could track their movements, anticipate their actions, exploit their weaknesses, and use the element of surprise to a devastating effect. They anticipated a nobleman, vulnerable and desperate, cowering in fear. They would find, instead, a predator, a beast unleashed, prepared to defend his mate with lethal force.

But the most crucial and agonizing piece of this intricate puzzle was Emily's safety. The manor, while seemingly an ordinary, if opulent, residence, was, in reality, a fortress, fortified with layers of security, both technological and arcane, secrets known only to me and passed down through generations of my family.

The servants, fiercely loyal and discreet, would act as an additional layer of protection, their watchful eyes and unwavering dedication ensuring her safety while I dealt with the immediate threat at the docks. Keeping her away, ignorant of the danger, despite the wrenching, visceral pain it caused me, was the only way to guarantee her survival.

Reaching the workshop, I threw myself into the task, my paws moving with a feverish, almost frantic precision. Every gear, every wire, every meticulously crafted component was a testament to my love for Emily, a step closer to ensuring her safety, a weapon forged in the crucible of my desperation.

The setting sun, a fiery orb sinking below the horizon, painted the sky with streaks of crimson and gold, the light filtering through my workshop's dusty, grimy windows, a stark reminder of the dwindling time. I had mere hours. I needed to complete the replica pendant, prepare the sonic devices, and reach the docks well before the appointed hour to set my trap.

$\mathcal{E}$mily

I didn't *want* a bath. Not really. But Nora had been insistent, and I, still reeling from the abruptness of Nathaniel's departure, had given in.

The water, heavily scented with lavender, lapped against my skin, a soothing balm that did little to ease the simmering unease that had taken root deep in my belly.

I lingered, swirling the fragrant, iridescent bubbles around my fingers, trying and failing to dispel the growing certainty that something was terribly, terribly wrong. He'd left so suddenly, a fleeting shadow of worry, or was it fear darkening his eyes? He'd claimed it was a business matter, but the lie had been pathetically transparent, a flimsy, threadbare curtain hastily drawn to conceal something far more sinister.

And that was the core of my distress. Not the lie itself, but the *need* for it. Did he truly believe me so fragile, so incapable of understanding, of *sharing* the burdens he carried?

Had I somehow given him the impression that I was a delicate, wilting flower, incapable of facing the harsh realities of his world?

Or was this simply his nature, the ingrained behavior of a creature of shadows and secrets, a being who instinctively kept even those closest to him at arm's length? The thought gnawed at me, a cold, hard knot of resentment tightening in my chest. We'd shared an intimacy, a connection that had felt profound, unbreakable, and yet, in a heartbeat, he'd erected a wall between us, a barrier of silence and deception.

I sighed, sinking deeper into the water, the lavender scent now cloying, almost suffocating. *Had I done something wrong?* Uttered some careless word, committed some unforgivable faux pas? The insidious whisper of self-doubt, a persistent irritant, threatened to erode the fragile foundation of my confidence. We'd been *so close*, so exquisitely intertwined, and then, with a swiftness that left me breathless, he'd withdrawn, leaving me adrift in a turbulent sea of uncertainty and hurt.

Nora, ever efficient, ever watchful, helped me into a fresh gown, her hands deft and practiced as she fastened the laces. I attempted, subtly, I hoped, to glean some information from her, some hint of Nathaniel's whereabouts, some clue as to the nature of his sudden departure. But her expression remained carefully neutral, her lips sealed in a perfect, infuriatingly polite line.

The other servants, too, were tight-lipped, their loyalty to Nathaniel absolute and unwavering. They offered polite smiles, evasive answers, their silence a solid, impenetrable wall that I couldn't breach no matter how hard I tried.

Descending the grand staircase, I found the dining room vast and deserted.

A single, opulent place setting awaited me, the silver gleaming coldly under the soft, diffused glow of the chandeliers. The aroma of freshly baked bread and sizzling bacon, usually a welcome invitation, filled the air, a tantalizing feast laid out for one.

I picked at my food, the usually delicious flavors turning to ash in my mouth. He wasn't here. He hadn't even waited to share a simple meal with me.

The absence of his presence was a palpable void, a gaping hole in the fabric of my morning.

A flicker of anger, sharp and defiant, ignited within me, chasing away the lingering tendrils of self-doubt. This wasn't about *me*. This was about *him*, about his ingrained, almost suffocatingly over-protective nature, his misguided belief that he could shield me from whatever darkness lurked beyond the gilded cage of his manor. He believed he could keep me locked away, safe and oblivious, while he faced the threats alone, a solitary knight battling unseen demons. He was *wrong*.

I pushed away my plate, the remnants of my uneaten food a testament to my growing unease. I wouldn't wait here, a passive princess imprisoned in a luxurious tower. I *would* find him. I *would* discover the truth and face it with him, side by side, regardless of the consequences. He might be a powerful lord, a creature of immense strength and ancient lineage, but I was a determined woman, armed with a fierce love and an unwavering resolve.

The oppressive silence of the manor, once a comfort, now felt suffocating, a tangible weight pressing down on me. Restlessness gnawed at me, a caged animal pacing frantically within the confines of my gilded prison. I needed air, space, a moment to breathe, to think, and to *plan*. Slipping out of the dining room, I made my way to the gardens, the heady scent of roses and honeysuckle a fragile, fleeting balm against the rising tide of my anxiety.

Nora, ever vigilant, trailed a discreet distance behind me, her presence a constant, almost palpable reminder of Nathaniel's protective, controlling hold. I strolled along the meticulously manicured paths, my eyes scanning the vibrant, almost aggressively cheerful flowerbeds, feigning admiration for the perfectly arranged blooms while my mind raced, desperately searching for answers, a way out, and a way to *him*.

A glint of white, a stark contrast to the deep green of the foliage, caught my eye. Tucked beneath a sprawling rose bush, partially concealed by a scattering of fallen leaves, lay a crumpled piece of paper.

My heart leaped, and with a quick, furtive glance over my shoulder to ensure Nora wasn't watching, I swiftly, almost instinctively, scooped up the discarded note, tucking it deep into the folds of my skirt, my fingers brushing against the soft fabric, a tangible link to the danger that awaited.

My hands trembled, almost uncontrollably, as I unfolded the paper, my breath catching in my throat, a strangled gasp as I read the chilling, brutal words. The blood drained from my face, leaving me cold, numb, and breathless. It wasn't business. It was a threat, a demand, a *ransom note* with *my* name on it, a stark, terrifying confirmation of my worst fears. And Nathaniel, that stubborn, infuriatingly overprotective wolf, had gone to face them *alone*.

A wave of anger—hot, fierce, and righteous—washed over me, eclipsing the fear. He thought he could protect me by keeping me in the dark, sacrificing himself, and offering himself up as a shield. He *underestimated* me. He failed to understand that I wasn't a fragile flower, a delicate bloom to be sheltered from the storm. I was a force to be reckoned with, a survivor, forged in the fires of adversity, and I *would not* let him face this alone.

The docks. 2 a.m. The words burned into my memory, a stark, unavoidable call to action. I needed a plan, a strategy, a way to slip past Nora's watchful gaze, to escape this gilded cage, and to reach the docks before Nathaniel made some reckless, irreversible decision. Escape wouldn't be easy, but I was resourceful, determined, and fueled by a love that burned brighter, fiercer, than any fear.

Nathaniel might believe he could protect me by keeping me locked away, but I was about to prove him utterly and devastatingly wrong. He was going to face this danger, yes, but he *wasn't* going to face it alone.

*E*mily

The opulent walls of my room, once a comforting embrace, now pressed in, suffocating me. *Confined?* Never. Nathaniel's overprotective charade had reached its limit. Anger, a tight, burning coil, vibrated through me with every restless stride across the plush, ridiculously expensive carpet. He underestimated me, *grossly* underestimated me, if he thought he could keep me safe, keep me *docile*, by locking me away like some fragile doll.

As twilight bled into the inky blackness of night, I slipped from my room, my heart beating frantically against my ribs. The familiar corridors, usually a source of comfort and quiet elegance, now felt oppressive, menacing, each creak of the ancient floorboards amplifying my growing anxiety, a soundtrack to my rebellion.

Nora, thankfully, was nowhere to be seen. I moved like a wraith, a ghost in my borrowed finery, the whisper of silk and lace against my skin a stark, almost mocking contrast to the turmoil raging within me.

The gardens lay cloaked in an eerie, unsettling stillness, the rustling leaves the only sound in the vast, echoing emptiness. The wrought-iron gates, usually imposing, symbols of wealth and security, now felt like the bars of a cage, a gilded prison designed to keep me contained. With a deep, shuddering breath, I slipped through a side gate, its protesting, rusty groan a deafening shriek in the quiet night.

The cold, unforgiving bite of cobblestones against my thin slippers sent a jolt of fear, sharp and immediate, through me. The darkness clung to everything, thick and suffocating, the shadows twisting and writhing into menacing shapes that danced and leered at the periphery of my vision. Icy dread, a wave of pure, unadulterated terror, washed over me.

Reckless, foolish, and utterly insane venturing out

alone.

The thought slammed into me with the force of a physical blow, but turning back was unthinkable, impossible. I'd come too far.

I turned left, the unfamiliar road a dark, treacherous ribbon unwinding before me into the unknown. My senses were on high alert, every rustle, every creak, every fleeting shadow a potential threat, my heart pounding a frantic tattoo against my ribs. I pressed on, breath snagged in my throat, a silent, desperate prayer my only companion in this terrifying, self-imposed exile.

A gruff voice, guttural and alien, shattered the silence, slicing through the night like a rusty blade. "Stumbled out of your nest?"

I whirled around, hand flying to my throat, a strangled gasp escaping my lips. A small, wiry figure emerged from the concealing shadows, moonlight illuminating sharp, angular features, a face that seemed carved from granite. Her eyes, like chips of obsidian, gleamed with an unsettling, predatory intensity. A *goblin.*

"Who..." I stammered, the word barely a whisper, a fragile thread of sound lost in the night's vastness.

"Thistle," she rasped, her voice like gravel grinding on stone, a sound that set my teeth on edge.

"And you're bleedin' lucky I found ya before somethin' *nastier* did."

Help? From a *goblin*?

The sheer absurdity of it struck me, a flicker of dark humor in the face of overwhelming fear. Yet, in the depths of her sharp, assessing gaze, I detected a flicker of… concern? It was fleeting, quickly masked by a practiced indifference, but it was *there*, enough to ignite a tiny, fragile sliver of hope in the fear that threatened to consume me.

"Bogrot sent me," Thistle explained, spitting on the cobblestones with a casual disdain that somehow made her seem even more dangerous. "He's got a nose for trouble, that one, sharper than any hound's. Smells somethin' rotten with these shadows. Doesn't want 'em gettin' too big for their britches. Heard Nathaniel was tanglin' with 'em, figured his little human pet might need a minder."

Relief, swift and intense, washed over me, quickly followed by a surge of renewed determination, a fierce resolve that burned away the lingering fear.

"I need to find him," I said, my voice still trembling, but stronger now, infused with a newfound purpose.

My gaze drifted upward, drawn to the luminous orb dominating the night sky, a silent, watchful presence. "The moon is full," I murmured, a sudden, unsettling thought, a chilling premonition, taking root in my mind. Had I been here that long? A whole month had passed quickly than I thought possible.

"Nah, day after," Thistle corrected, jerking her chin toward the moon, its edge slightly, almost imperceptibly, diminished. "Wanin', she is." I rubbed my shoulder, my fingers tracing the faint, lingering marks beneath the fabric of my gown. The words from Nathaniel's dusty, leather-bound books about lunar cycles and their potent, unpredictable effects flashed through my mind. *Could it be? Could I change? He was the one cursed, not me.* The thought was terrifying, exhilarating, utterly impossible, and yet…

"Right, then," Thistle interrupted my spiraling, increasingly frantic thoughts, cracking her knuckles with a sharp, unsettling sound. "I'm a tracker, best this side of the Whispering Woods. Let's see if we can sniff out where your wolf has gone a-wanderin'."

CHAPTER 20

*L*ord Nathaniel Blackwood

The salt-laced air, thick with the stench of brine and decay, whipped at my face, a brutal reminder of the precariousness of my situation. The rhythmic slap of waves against the docks' barnacle-encrusted pilings echoed the frantic, uneven beat of my heart, a hectic drumbeat of impending doom.

A fleeting, agonizingly vivid image of Emily flashed through my mind—her radiant smile, the way her eyes, the color of warm honey, sparkled with an irrepressible joy—a painful, almost unbearable reminder of everything I stood to lose, everything I was fighting to protect.

My plan, conceived in haste and fueled by a desperate hope, had seemed so deceptively simple. Lure the shadows with the meticulously crafted fake pendant, flush out the puppeteer, and expose the mastermind pulling the strings of this elaborate, deadly game.

The fake pendant, its cold, inert metal, pulsed with a faint, almost imperceptible energy. A pale imitation of the true artifact's power, and a reflection of my growing unease. Shadows, drawn to the illusion like moths to a flickering, dying flame, writhed and coalesced around me, their forms shifting and swirling, obscuring the already dim moonlight.

I braced myself, muscles coiled tight, senses hyperalert, every nerve ending screaming a silent warning. A prickle of unease, a primal instinct honed over centuries, crawled up my spine. The air crackled, thick with an unseen, malevolent energy, a palpable tension that squeezed the air from my lungs, making each breath a labored effort.

Then, a blinding flash, a supernova of white-hot agony that ripped through me, stealing my breath, leaving me gasping, choking on the sudden, over-whelming pain. A metallic tang, the coppery, unmistakable taste of blood, flooded my mouth, mingling with the salty spray of the sea. I staggered back, my senses reeling, the world tilting precariously on its axis, threatening to plunge me into darkness. The meticulously crafted fake pendant, now reduced to a useless, glittering powder, crumbled in my hand, symbolizing my shattered plan.

As my vision swam back into focus, blurred and distorted, they emerged from the swirling shadows—Malcolm and Eleanor. Their faces, once so familiar, so seemingly trustworthy, were twisted into grotesque masks of triumphant malice, a horrifying parody of their former selves. How could they be the ones behind the control of the shadows?

Malcolm's eyes, once warm and filled with a jovial light, now burned with a cold, predatory intensity, the gaze of a hunter who had finally cornered his prey. Eleanor's lips, usually curved into a gentle, almost ethereal smile, were stretched into a thin, cruel line, revealing a hint of sharp, almost feral teeth.

The betrayal hit me not as a physical blow, but as a sickening, hollow emptiness in the very core of my being, a cold wave of nausea and despair washing over me, threatening to drown me in its icy depths. My stomach clenched, a cold sweat slicking my skin, a physical manifestation of the horror that gripped me.

"You…" I rasped, the word a broken whisper, a

strangled cry of disbelief and fury warring in my throat.

Malcolm chuckled, a chilling, hollow sound that echoed the relentless lapping of the waves against the pilings, sending a shiver of pure dread down my spine.

"Remember that time we fought the wraiths in the Whispering Woods, Nathaniel?" he asked, his voice dripping with a false, mocking nostalgia, each word a poisoned barb aimed at my heart. "You saved my life that day, risked everything for me. Funny, isn't it, how things turn out? How easily loyalty can be twisted, corrupted…"

"Why?" I choked out, the word raw and ragged, torn from the depths of my despair.

Eleanor stepped forward, her movements fluid and graceful, yet imbued with a terrifying, predatory power. Her eyes blazed with a disturbing, almost otherworldly fanaticism, her pupils contracting into thin, vertical slits, like those of a serpent. A faint, yet unmistakable, sulfurous odor emanated from her, the acrid stench of something ancient and profoundly malevolent, something that whispered of dark rituals and forbidden knowledge.

"Time travel, Nathaniel," she hissed, her voice taking on a strange, resonant quality, a voice that seemed to vibrate with an unnatural power.

"Imagine the possibilities! The sheer, unadulterated *power*! The world, *history itself*, will be ours to mold, reshape, and *perfect* as we see fit!"

They weren't just power-hungry, they were utterly delusional, consumed by a dangerous, all-consuming fantasy, a madness that threatened to unravel the very fabric of reality. A wave of icy terror, a premonition of unimaginable horror, washed over me, a chilling certainty gripping my heart.

Enchanted ropes, pulsing with a dark, viscous energy that seemed to writhe and twist of their own accord, bit into my wrists, searing my flesh like burning coals, the agonizing pain a sharp, insistent reminder of my utter helplessness. The scent of burning flesh, my flesh, filled the air. They dragged me, helpless and bleeding, toward a derelict warehouse, its crumbling façade looming like a skeletal maw in the darkness, the air thick with the cloying smell of mildew, decay, and the acrid stench of rat droppings.

"She's the key, Eleanor," Malcolm said, his voice low and urgent, a conspiratorial whisper that sent another wave of dread washing over me. "Emily. She holds the *true* power of the pendant within her, dormant, waiting to be awakened."

Eleanor's eyes glittered with a predatory,

ravenous hunger, a terrifying anticipation that made my blood run cold. "And we will *take* it," she snarled, her voice laced with a chilling, possessive lust, a promise of unspeakable horrors to come.

Each word was a shard of ice piercing my heart, shattering my soul. My desperate attempts to protect Emily and shield her from the encroaching darkness had, with cruel and devastating irony, paved the path straight to her doom.

A low, guttural growl, a sound that was neither fully human nor entirely beast, echoed from the oppressive shadows of the warehouse, a promise of further torment. Then, a raspy and ancient voice that seemed to claw its way out of the very depths of hell, whispered from the darkness, "The game, my dear Nathaniel, has only *just* begun."

*E*mily

The cold, damp air of the warehouse, thick with the scent of mildew and rust, pressed against my skin like a suffocating shroud. Each ragged breath I took echoed in the cavernous space, a stark counterpoint to the frantic hammering of my heart.

Thistle's wiry hand gripped my arm, her claws digging in slightly, a painful anchor in the swirling chaos. The metallic tang of fear, sharp and bitter, coated my tongue.

"Malcolm," Thistle hissed, her voice a rasp of gravel against my ear, her head tilted toward a figure whose cruel smirk I could just make out in the dim light filtering through the grimy, cobweb-draped windows. "And Eleanor. Look, that ruby choker. The one she wore the night Lord Elbridge died. Remember the whispers? That she *drained* him, left him a withered husk?" Her voice dropped to a bare whisper, a thread of sound lost in the vastness. "Councilman Thorne. Baroness Von Hess. They're all *here*, Emily. Deeper in this... this *rot...* than I ever imagined."

My breath hitched, a strangled gasp caught in my throat. Thorne, his face a mask of avarice and ambition, I recognized from my father's endless research gatherings. He'd always been there, whispering in my father's ear, pushing him toward ruthless, morally bankrupt business practices. Von Hess, her eyes glittering with a cold, predatory hunger, I recalled seeing at the opera, dripping in jewels. But it was the sight of *Nathaniel*, bound tightly to a central pillar, his head slumped forward, his body bearing the marks of their cruelty, that sent a jolt of pure, icy terror through me, a wave of nausea threatening to overwhelm me.

My chest *ached*, a constricting band of pain making each breath a labored effort. My hands curled into fists, nails digging crescents into my palms, a physical manifestation of the rage and desperation building within me.

I have to get to him.

"Emily, we have to go," Thistle urged, her voice tight with a desperate anxiety that mirrored mine. Her claws dug into my arm as she tugged, trying to pull me back toward the relative safety of the shadows. "This is suicide. We're outnumbered, outmatched…"

"I won't leave him," I whispered, my voice trembling, but resolute. *I won't.*

A wave of dizziness washed over me, but through the haze, I saw Nathaniel shift, his head lifting, his eyes meeting mine. Even bound and vulnerable, he radiated a strength, a silent promise that anchored me.

I have to do this. For him. For us.

The pendant pulsed against my palm, a frantic rhythm. I stepped out of the shadows, the faint light glinting off the dust motes. I lifted my chin, forcing a steadiness into my voice that I didn't feel. *Don't show fear.*

Malcolm's sneer deepened. "Well, well," he drawled, the cruel amusement in his voice making my stomach churn. "The little bird walks right into the cage. How convenient."

"I'm here for Nathaniel," I said, my voice still trembling, but I met his gaze, refusing to look away.

A tall man, his face a canvas of sharp angles and deep shadows, stepped forward.

"Foolish girl," His voice was a low hum, vibrating in the air. He gestured dismissively around the cavernous warehouse. "This… this *decay…* is all that remains of the Corvus legacy. My family, once masters of this city, reduced to *this*," he spat out, the sound sharp.

"Silas, go easy." Eleanor, her ruby choker pulsing, gave a sharp nod. "While *others…*" she said, her gaze flicking to Nathaniel, "… bask in unearned privilege." Her voice dripped venom.

Malcolm stepped closer, his face inches from mine. I could smell whiskey and something else. Something *dark* and wrong. "The Blackwoods…" he hissed. "They stole everything." He brushed the pendant with his fingers, and I flinched back, a gasp escaping my lips.

"Careful, Malcolm," Silas warned, his voice silken. "The girl is… fragile. For now." He turned his cold gaze back to me. "Give it to me," he commanded. "And perhaps your pet will be spared."

My fingers tightened around the pendant. *No.* I glanced at Nathaniel, his eyes filled with pain and fear. For *me*? The sight fueled a desperate courage.

Silas raised a hand, and the shadows around us *shifted*, pressing closer, a suffocating weight. The air grew thick, heavy with a palpable malevolence, and a low, guttural hum resonated through the warehouse, vibrating in my bones. Tendrils of darkness snaked across the floor, reaching for me. The smell of ozone, sharp and acrid, burned my nostrils.

"They hunger," Silas whispered, his breath cold against my ear. "They feed on the energy of those who have traversed time. You are a feast they've long awaited."

My heart hammered. "What… what do you mean?" I stammered.

"The pendant," he whispered. "It is the key. And we are ready to unlock its power."

Desperation clawed at me. I couldn't let them use Nathaniel or me. The shadows pressed closer, their icy touch searing my skin. I closed my eyes, picturing my mother's face, her loving smile.

I have to do something.

Then I remembered Nathaniel's explanation of the pendant's volatile nature, its potential for destruction.

A desperate gamble, but my only chance.

My hand tightened on the pendant, my nails digging into my palm.

"Thistle…" I whispered, my voice barely audible, "… get Nathaniel out of here. *Now.*"

Before Thistle could react, before the shadows

could fully consume me, I lifted the pendant, its light flaring one last time. It was a brilliant, defiant flash that illuminated the faces of those around me—Malcolm's sneer, Eleanor's calculating gaze, the tall man's predatory grin, all momentarily frozen in expressions of shock and disbelief. Then, with a guttural cry, a scream of defiance and despair born of love and desperation, I slammed the pendant against the cracked, concrete floor.

The explosion was blinding, deafening, a cataclysmic release of raw, untamed energy. A shock wave ripped through the warehouse, throwing me back against the cold, damp stone, the force of the blast knocking the wind out of me.

The air crackled, alive with power. The shadows *shrieked*, a chorus of tortured, otherworldly wails as they recoiled from the blast, their forms dissolving, dissipating into wisps of smoke that curled and twisted before vanishing entirely, leaving behind only the lingering scent of ozone and the echo of their screams.

Then, silence.

A heavy, ringing silence, broken only by the sound of my ragged breathing. Dust rained down from the rafters, coating everything in a fine gray film, a ghostly shroud. A large section of the roof had collapsed, letting in a sliver of cold, indifferent moonlight, a stark contrast to the warm glow of the now-shattered pendant.

The remnants of the pendant lay scattered around me, glittering shards of crystal and metal in the dust. I had made my choice, a choice born of love and sacrifice. But at what cost?

Nathaniel stirred, groaning softly, a sound that was both agonizing and hopeful. Hope, fragile and tentative, flickered within me, a tiny flame in the darkness. The warehouse walls still loomed, imposing and menacing, but now, cracks spider-webbed across their surface, a sign of their weakened state. Perhaps, just perhaps, we had a *chance*.

CHAPTER 22

*L*ord Nathaniel Blackwood

The pendant shattered with a sound like the breaking of a world, the explosion echoing in the sudden, stunned silence. The shadows, moments before a suffocating presence, recoiled as if struck, their inky forms twisting, shrieking, and dissipating into wisps of acrid smoke that stung my eyes. Pain, sharp and immediate, lanced through me, a searing reminder of my wounds.

Then, a glint of steel—Thistle, signaling from the shadows, her face a mask of grim determination. *Emily!* My heart leaped with desperate hope, quickly followed by a surge of terror. *She was here?* Before I could even process the thought, all hell broke loose.

A raw, guttural cry, a war cry that resonated deep within my bones, ripped through the silence. From the darkness beyond the feeble pools of lamplight, a figure erupted. Bogrot, Raziel's personal guard, his eyes blazing with a fierce, almost feral light. He carried a wickedly curved scimitar, its edge glinting, and a primal snarl twisted his lips. He wasn't alone.

A deafening crack, like thunder splitting the sky, rocked the warehouse. Dust, splinters, and debris rained down. The force of the blast slammed me back against the rough, splintered floor, stealing my breath. I tasted blood, my own, and the acrid tang of smoke and something else… ozone and goblin musk.

Goblins.

Goblins were swarming the warehouse, seemingly materializing from the shadows themselves, a tide of green skin and flashing steel. Their movements were swift and brutal, a coordinated whirlwind of slashing blades, guttural snarls, and terrifying efficiency. They moved differently from the shadows, grounded, *real,* a stark contrast to the ethereal darkness.

I struggled to rise, my head swimming, my body screaming in protest. I had to get to Emily. I had to protect her. But the ropes still held me fast.

Then, I saw her. Emily. She was moving toward me, a shard of the shattered pendant clutched in her hand, her face pale but determined. One of the shadows, disoriented by the explosion and the goblin onslaught, stumbled away from me, its form flickering.

Now or never.

"Emily!" I gasped, my voice hoarse, but she was already lunging forward, slashing at the enchanted ropes binding my wrists.

I cried out as the shard grazed my skin, a sharp, stinging pain, but the ropes, weakened by the pendant's destruction, parted. I pulled myself free, my eyes locking with hers, a mixture of relief, gratitude, and sheer terror flooding through me.

Just as I moved to shield her, a shadow, its form solidifying, lunged at her, a dark, swirling mass of energy aimed at her chest. Without thinking, I shoved her aside, taking the brunt of the attack myself.

Pain exploded through me, a searing agony that stole my breath. I crumpled to the ground, clutching my side, a dark, crimson stain blossoming rapidly across my shirt. *Not again.* I could feel myself slipping, the darkness closing in.

I heard the sounds of battle raging around me—the clash of steel, the goblins' guttural snarls, and the shrieks of the dissolving shadows. A small but lightning-fast goblin darted past, its blade slicing through the legs of a towering shadow. Another leaped onto a crate, spitting a stream of vile, hissing acid. Bogrot, roaring with savage glee, plunged his curved scimitar into the chest of the tall man, Silas, the leader. The blade sank deep with a sickening thud. Silas crumpled, his body dissolving into nothingness.

The fight, though brutal, was short-lived. With their ferocity and unexpected arrival, the goblins had turned the tide. As the authorities, alerted by the explosion, finally arrived, I saw Malcolm and Eleanor being led away in chains, their faces contorted with rage and disbelief.

Bogrot, his task complete, his chest heaving, his green skin slick with sweat and the dark ichor of the shadows, offered me a curt nod. "Lord Blackwood," he rumbled, a flicker of respect in his fiery gaze. He then melted back into the shadows with his contingent as quickly and silently as they had appeared.

Thistle emerged, her face grim. "Are you all right, Lord Blackwood?" she asked. I managed a weak nod, my gaze searching frantically for Emily.

"Emily?" I croaked, my voice barely a whisper.

"She's here," Thistle said, stepping aside.

Emily rushed to my side, her face pale and

streaked with tears, her hands trembling as she reached for me. "Nathaniel! Oh God, Nathaniel…"

Thistle kneeled beside me, her skilled hands probing my wound. "He'll live," she pronounced. "It's deep, but not fatal. He needs rest." She looked at Emily, her expression softening. "Take care of him." With a final nod, she left us.

The return to the mansion was a blur. I remember the rhythmic clip-clop of the horses' hooves, the gentle rocking of the carriage, and Emily holding me close, her hand pressed against my wound, trying to staunch the flow of blood. Her touch and presence were the only things that kept me tethered to consciousness.

In my chambers, the soft glow of the lamps casting long shadows, Emily kneeled beside me as I lay on the bed, my face pale and drawn, my breathing shallow. "Emily …" I began, my voice hoarse, "… you shouldn't have… sacrificed your future… for me. Your life…"

"I had to," she interrupted, her gaze locking with mine, her voice soft but resolute. "There was no other choice. Because…"

My paw, weak but warm, reached out, finding hers. "Emily…" I whispered, my voice thick with emotion. *I love you.* The words were there on the tip of my tongue, but I couldn't quite voice them yet.

She leaned closer. "Nathaniel," she whispered, her fingers tracing the edge of the bandage.

I whimpered softly, a low, pained sound. *God, I was weak.* But her eyes, filled with a vulnerability that mirrored mine, held me captive.

"I shouldn't have put you in danger," I murmured, the self-recrimination a bitter taste in my mouth.

"You didn't," she replied, her voice catching. "I chose to be there. I chose to fight. Because…" Her gaze met mine, unwavering. "Because I love you, Nathaniel. I love you with all my heart."

The words, spoken with such fierce conviction, sent a wave of warmth through me, chasing away the lingering chill of the shadows. I shifted slightly, wincing in pain, and with a gentle tug, pulled her closer until my head rested in her lap. She stroked my fur, her touch soothing, calming.

"I love you, too, Emily," I whispered, the words a raw, heartfelt confession, my breath warm against her skin.

I nudged her hand with my wet nose, a low, rumbling growl vibrating in my chest, a sound that was both a plea and a promise. She leaned in, and I met her halfway, pressing a kiss to her lips, a soft, tentative touch that deepened into something profound.

My large body, still in its part wolf form,

enveloped her in its warmth. She ran her fingers through my thick, soft fur, and I felt a sense of peace, of belonging that I'd never known before.

The night was filled with the scent of musk and moonlight, the soft rustle of fur against skin, the silent language of love. In this moment, in her embrace, I found complete acceptance of the monster I was.

CHAPTER 23

*L*ord Nathaniel Blackwood

The sun, a warmth on my back, eased the lingering ache in my muscles, a physical reminder of the battles fought and won. Beside me, Emily's hand, small and warm within mine, sent a comforting, electric jolt through me with every swing of our joined arms. The cobblestone path, dappled with the intricate shadows of leaves dancing in the gentle breeze, felt solid and real beneath my feet, an anchor to the present.

The city, once cloaked in a preternatural gloom, a suffocating blanket of fear, now vibrated with the cheerful, almost defiant hum of normalcy. The shadow-slingers were gone, their oppressive presence replaced by the sweet, intoxicating scent of roses and freshly turned earth, a promise of renewal.

I inhaled deeply, the fragrant air a balm to my still-healing body, a tangible representation of the peace we had fought for. The garden, bursting with vibrant colors, a riot of life, felt like a testament to resilience, a stark contrast to the darkness we'd faced.

With Emily beside me, her presence a constant, unwavering source of strength and love, I felt not just healed but reborn. Being close to her, truly close, in this newfound peace, it *almost* felt as if the invisible barrier of the curse had momentarily receded, a sensation like finally coming home, like exhaling after holding my breath for far too long.

"Are you *sure* you're up for this?" Emily asked, her playful smile unable to fully mask the concern that flickered in her eyes, eyes that shimmered like sunlight on water, reflecting the depths of her love and worry. Her touch, light as a butterfly's wing, a fleeting caress against my arm, sent a shiver down my spine, a mixture of pleasure and a lingering unease.

I chuckled, a low rumble in my chest, but a twinge in my side, a phantom pain, belied my words. "Fine as ever," I lied, squeezing her hand reassuringly, wanting to reassure myself as much as her, to banish the lingering shadows of doubt. "And besides, a peaceful morning stroll with *you* is a precious thing, a treasure I won't squander."

We rounded a bend in the path, Lady Beatrice, her silver hair catching the sunlight like a halo, a beacon of warmth, beamed at us, her face alight with genuine affection.

"Nathaniel! Emily! Magnificent! Simply *magnificent*! You were both so brave, so incredibly courageous," she gushed, her words tumbling over each other in her excitement, her enthusiasm infectious. "Thank you, from the bottom of my heart, for ridding us of that dreadful, terrifying menace."

"It was our pleasure, Lady Beatrice," I replied, the warmth of her praise spreading through me, a welcome balm after the long weeks of fear, tension, and the constant, gnawing presence of the curse. "Though we had some unexpected and very welcome help."

"Indeed! You two are quite the pair, a force to be reckoned with." She chuckled, her laughter light and musical, echoing the joy in my heart. "Dinner at my estate soon? We *must* celebrate this victory, this new beginning!"

Similar greetings and congratulations followed from Mr. Ellsworth, the usually boisterous bookseller, his voice filled with genuine gratitude, and even the reserved Mrs. Cavendish, the librarian, her usually stern face softened with relief and a hint of admiration. The outpouring of gratitude from the community was both heartwarming and humbling, a stark contrast to the isolation and *loneliness* I'd felt while cursed and trapped within my wolf form.

Lord Maxwell, his normally stern features softened with relief, his eyes surprisingly gentle, boomed, "Nathaniel, my boy! A service to us all! Unparalleled courage! You and Emily are an inspiration, a testament to the power of love and bravery." He clapped me heartily on the shoulder, his grip firm but careful, mindful of my recent injury. "Dinner at my estate this Friday? A toast is in order! To your health, to your happiness, and to your future!"

Emily's eyes sparkled with delight. "We'd be delighted, Lord Maxwell," she accepted, her voice ringing with genuine pleasure, her hand squeezing mine in a silent expression of shared joy.

As the crowd dispersed, their well-wishes echoing in the air, Thistle approached, her small frame radiating an almost preternatural confidence, a quiet strength that belied her size. Beside her stood her imposing master and Morwen, the witch. My pulse quickened, a sudden, unexpected flutter of anxiety in my chest. *This was it.* The moment of truth.

"Thistle," I greeted, my voice strained with anticipation and a deep-seated, almost primal fear.

"Nathaniel," she replied, her eyes gleaming with a mischievous spark, a hint of something unreadable. "Morwen has something to discuss with you. Privately."

My stomach clenched, a knot of apprehension tightening in my gut. Despite the warmth of the sun on my skin and Emily's comforting presence beside me, a cold dread, a whisper of the past, seeped into my bones. The curse had been a part of me for so long, a defining characteristic, a shackle that had also, in a strange way, become a shield.

Thistle led us to a secluded alcove, hidden from the bustling activity of the main garden path by a thick wall of flowering vines. The air here was still and quiet, heavy with the scent of blossoms and damp earth, the only sound the gentle rustling of leaves in the nearby trees, a soothing counterpoint to the turmoil within me. Morwen turned to me, her gaze intense, penetrating, yet surprisingly gentle, a depth of understanding in her eyes that both unnerved and comforted me.

"Nathaniel," her voice, smooth as polished obsidian, yet resonant with an unexpected warmth, resonated with a power that seemed to vibrate in the very air around us. "I have come to offer you a choice. A release. You have proven yourself worthy. You have shown that the beast within is not your master, that you have the strength to control it, to choose love over darkness. You risked your life, your very *being*, for Emily and for the innocent. You have earned your freedom."

A wave of emotion, so intense it nearly buckled my knees, crashed over me. Relief, yes, a profound, overwhelming sense of liberation, but also fear. Disbelief. A flicker of apprehension, a whisper of doubt. The curse had been a part of me for so long, a defining characteristic, a constant companion. It felt strange, *wrong*, to imagine life without it. Who was I without the wolf?

"Truly free?" I whispered, my voice choked with emotion, the words barely audible. The question was not just about the physical transformation, but about the *internal* one. Could I truly be free of the darkness that had haunted me for so long?

"Truly," she confirmed, her gaze unwavering, her voice firm and reassuring. "The curse will be lifted, but it requires your willing acceptance, your *conscious* choice. You must embrace the change, embrace the man you are meant to be, without the shadow of the wolf hanging over you."

I looked at Emily, her hand a comforting, grounding anchor in mine, her love my guide in the swirling chaos of my emotions. The weight of the past, a heavy, suffocating burden I had carried for so long, seemed to momentarily lift, replaced by a glimmer of hope, a promise of a future I had never dared to dream of. Looking into her eyes, seeing the unwavering love and belief reflected there, I knew I was ready. I *had* to be.

"I accept," I stated, my voice firm, resolute, a declaration of intent. The words echoed in the quiet alcove, a promise to myself, Emily, and the future.

Morwen raised her hands, her long, slender fingers glowing with a faint, ethereal light. Her lips moved in a silent incantation, a whisper of ancient words, a language I didn't understand but felt deep within my bones.

A tingling warmth spread from my toes, flowing upward, enveloping me in a wave of energy, a sensation both exhilarating and terrifying. My wolf form, usually a constant, simmering presence beneath my skin, *shimmered*, the dark fur seeming to absorb the strange, otherworldly light that emanated from Morwen's hands, a visible manifestation of the magic at work.

The phantom ache in my side, the last vestige of the shadow's attack, the lingering reminder of my vulnerability, dissolved completely, replaced by a feeling of wholeness, of *completeness*. I felt lighter and stronger, as if shackles I hadn't even realized I wore, chains forged of fear and self-doubt, had been shattered, leaving me free and unburdened.

A surge of raw power, exhilarating and terrifying in its intensity, coursed through me before fading, leaving me feeling cleansed, renewed, and profoundly *changed*. For the first time since the curse had taken hold, I felt whole. Truly, deeply whole. *Me*.

My form flickered, a dizzying, disorienting dance between human and wolf, a chaotic struggle for dominance. Then, with a surge of *will*, I focused, picturing my human form, *feeling* it solidify beneath my skin. My fur receded, my paws lengthening and reshaping into hands, the bones shifting and clicking into place with a strange, satisfying finality.

Morwen lowered her hands, the ethereal light fading, leaving behind only the soft glow of the afternoon sun filtering through the trees. "It is done," she declared, a genuine smile, a rare and precious gift, gracing her lips. "The curse is broken. You are free to shift between human and wolf at will."

Tears welled in Emily's eyes—tears of joy, relief, and overwhelming love. She threw her arms around me, her body pressed close to mine, a fierce, possessive embrace. The contact, now uninhibited by the curse's lingering effects, by the fear of the wolf, sent a jolt of pure, unadulterated desire through me, a powerful, primal connection.

I held her close, burying my face in her hair, inhaling her scent, a heady mix of lavender and something uniquely *her*, a scent that grounded me, that brought me home. Free.

"I preferred you as a wolf," she said, and I pulled away, searching her eyes which had a cheeky glint in them.

"It can be arranged."

I looked at Emily, my heart overflowing with a love so fierce and profound, it was almost a physical ache, a beautiful, overwhelming emotion.

I cupped her face in my hands, my thumbs gently wiping away her tears. "I couldn't do this with my paws."

Emily grinned at me. "I like your paws on me… and your hands, because they are both *you*."

"Let's go home, Emily." The word 'home' resonated with a new, deeper meaning, a sanctuary not just of walls and a roof, but of love, belonging, of a future shared, and a future *free*.

EPILOGUE

$\mathcal{E}$mily

The moon, a perfect silver disc, a celestial voyeur, hung heavy in the inky sky, casting an ethereal, almost *unreal* glow upon the manicured lawns and sculpted hedges of the mansion grounds. A gentle breeze, laden with the intoxicating perfume of night-blooming jasmine, damp earth, and something *wild* whispered through the leaves, a soothing counterpoint to my ear's frantic, almost painful hammering.

Tonight, under the watchful eye of this ancient witness, I would change. I would become a wolf for the first time.

Nathaniel stood beside me, a silent, reassuring presence, a solid anchor in the swirling sea of my anticipation. I could feel the tension radiating from him, a palpable wave of anxiety that mirrored my own, though his was tinged with guilt I refused to acknowledge, a burden he didn't need to carry. I saw the apology forming on his lips, the way his jaw tightened, his hand hovering near mine as if seeking permission to touch, comfort, and *ground* me.

"Emily, I—" he began, his voice a low murmur, thick with unspoken words, with regret and a love that transcended words.

"Don't," I interrupted gently, turning to face him, my hand finding his, squeezing reassuringly, a silent promise I needed him to understand. This wasn't a burden, not a sacrifice made for him. It was a *choice*, a step toward a shared future, a merging of our souls. "You don't need to apologize. This is… this is part of me *now*. A part I choose."

"But it's my fault," he insisted, his brow furrowed, his eyes, usually so bright, now dark with self-reproach that tore at my heart. "You shouldn't have to change, to become… a wolf… because of me."

"I have a feeling—" I cut him off again, a thrill of anticipation, a wild, almost reckless excitement, coursing through me, chasing away the last, lingering vestiges of fear, a fear that was quickly being replaced by something *powerful.* "That I'm going to *enjoy* this."

I met his gaze, my eyes shining with excitement, affection, and a hint of something *predatory.* "Becoming a werewolf, being *like* you... I think it will bring us closer, bind us together in a way nothing else could." A fleeting doubt, a whisper of fear—*what if I lose myself?*—flickered through me, but I pushed it down and embraced the unknown.

A flicker of hope and a spark of understanding ignited in his eyes, mirroring the burgeoning excitement and wildness within my soul. A small, hesitant smile, a promise of shared joy, played on his lips. "You really think so?"

"I *know* so," I replied, the conviction in my voice unwavering, a certainty that resonated deep within my bones. The first tremors of the transformation began to ripple through me, a tingling warmth spreading from my core, a low, almost painful hum vibrating beneath my skin. My bones felt like they were shifting, *liquefying,* and rearranging into something new, wild, and *powerful.*

The moonlight washed over us, a silver tide that seemed to shimmer and pulse with an otherworldly energy, a tangible manifestation of the magic at work. The air *crackled,* not just with anticipation but with the scent of ozone, pine needles crushed under-foot, and *wolf*. I could hear the whisper of the wind through the leaves with a clarity I'd never experienced before, the distant hoot of an owl, the rustle of a small creature in the undergrowth, sounds that had always been there, but now resonated with a new, vibrant intensity.

"Are you ready?" Nathaniel asked, his voice a low, guttural rumble that resonated deep within my chest, a vibration that echoed the changes within me. The concern was still there, a shadow in his eyes, but it was now overshadowed by a shared anticipation, a thrill of the unknown, a *hunger* for what was to come.

"More than ready," I whispered, closing my eyes, surrendering to the sensation, the power, and the *inevitability* of the change.

Then, the transformation began. A searing pain, like liquid fire, ripped through me, followed by an icy cold that stole my breath. My bones *cracked* and *shifted*, a sickening, grinding sound that echoed in my ears. Muscles I didn't know I possessed *contracted* and *expanded*, twisting and tearing, reshaping my body from the inside out.

A scream, raw and primal, tore from my throat, a sound I didn't recognize as my own, a cry of both agony and exhilaration? *Was this what it meant to be a wolf?* A fleeting thought, a whisper of fear—*am I losing myself?*—flickered through the pain, but it was quickly swallowed by the overwhelming tide of sensation.

And then stillness—a profound, almost unsettling quiet, broken only by the frantic hammering of my new heart. I opened my eyes, and the world *exploded* with color and scent.

The moonlight, no longer a soft glow, was a *blinding silver fire*, illuminating every blade of grass, every dewdrop with painful clarity. The air, thick with a thousand new scents, assaulted my nostrils, the rich, earthy smell of the forest floor, damp and teeming with life. The sharp, pungent scent of pine needles crushed under my paws. The sweet, musky scent of Nathaniel, now amplified, intoxicating, and the faint, metallic tang of my blood, a scent that both repulsed and strangely excited me.

My senses, *supercharged*, thrummed with a newfound awareness, a connection to the world around me that was both exhilarating and terrifying. I could *hear* the whisper of the wind through the leaves, the frantic scurrying of a mouse in the under-growth, the distant, mournful howl of another wolf —sounds that had always been there but now resonated with a depth and clarity I'd never imagined. I looked down at my hands, now *paws*, covered in thick, silver fur that shimmered in the moonlight. I lifted them, flexing my claws, *feeling* their sharpness, their lethal potential.

Raw and untamed power surged through me, a wild, exhilarating energy that made me want to *run, hunt, howl, and claim* this new world as my own. A flicker of fear—*what have I become?*—but it was quickly drowned out by the overwhelming tide of instinct, power, and *belonging*.

With his transformation complete, Nathaniel stood before me, magnificent in his wolf form, a creature of power and grace. His eyes, blazing with golden light, met mine, a look of pure, unadulterated love and *recognition*. He took a step closer, his powerful form radiating heat and a primal energy that resonated deep within me, a magnetic pull.

He nudged me with his wet nose, the touch sending a jolt of pure electricity through me, a spark that ignited a fire within. A low growl rumbled in his chest, a sound of possessiveness, claiming, and *belonging*.

I leaned into him, inhaling his scent, a heady mix of the forest, musk, and something uniquely *him*, a scent that was both familiar and intoxicatingly new. It was the scent of *home*.

He nipped playfully at my ear, a gentle, teasing

gesture, and I responded with a playful growl of my own, a sound that surprised me with its depth and resonance. We circled each other, testing, teasing, the air thick with a tension that was exciting and comforting, a primal dance of connection.

He seemed to *see* me, truly see me, not just the woman I had been, but the creature I had become. And in his eyes, I saw acceptance, love, and a shared wildness.

We ran. Our paws pounding the earth in a shared, synchronized rhythm, the wind whipping through our fur, a symphony of freedom.

The mansion faded into the distance. We were free, wild, and *together*, bound by something stronger than blood or magic. Bound by love.

Under the moon's watchful eye, we found our place, not just beside each other, but *within* each other, a merging of souls, a completion. This was more than a transformation. It was a *joining*, a melding of two beings into one, a perfect union of human and wolf.

And as I ran beside Nathaniel, our bodies moving in perfect synchronization, our breaths mingling in the night air, I knew this was just the beginning of our forever, a journey of love and wildness, of passion and companionship, forever bound by the magic of the moon, by the power of our shared wolf hearts.

The End

Check out more monster romance by Lilliana Rose:

ACKNOWLEDGMENTS

A huge thank you to Kaylene, Lisa, and Nikki for their expert eyes and editing skills in getting my story ready for publication.

To Kit, thank you for another wonderful cover – you've captured the essence of the story perfectly!

And of course, endless cuddles and a big, slobbery thank you to my furry writing assistant, Sprinkles, who keeps me company, reminds me to take breaks.

ABOUT THE AUTHOR

Lilliana Rose weaves enchanting tales of shifters, witches, and the monsters that lurk in the shadows of the unknown. Love ignites amidst the untamed wilderness, where ancient lore and cryptic prophecies whisper secrets of the past. When she's not conjuring thrilling plots, a quiet evening finds her curled up with a cup of tea (or a glass of red wine) and a book featuring a wolf or dragon on the cover. Lilliana brings a unique blend of logic and imagination to her writing, creating stories that will haunt your dreams and keep you spellbound until the very last page.

www.ingramcontent.com/pod-product-compliance
Lightning Source LLC
Chambersburg PA
CBHW060546190726

48283CB00003B/895